Jingle Bell Run
Pamela Seales

To: Griffisens
I am so thankful
for Bonnie and
Jim!

Pam Seales

For
Julia, Andy, and Jesse

Running to Your Dreams

Verse 1:
She was from a small town,
Out in the middle of nowhere,
Had a beat-up pickup, pockets full of quarters
And a dream to make it outta there
She was always singing

Chorus:
Set your soles on fire
Blaze ahead at full speed
Keep your faith alive
As you're running to your dreams

Verse 2:
Truck broke down halfway outta town
Right by the local five-and-dime,
She spent her last cent on a bottle of Ale 8,
And thought that maybe it just wasn't her time
But she couldn't help singing

Chorus:
Set your soles on fire
Blaze ahead at full speed
Keep your faith alive
As you're running to your dreams

Bridge:
Without a car she didn't think she could make it
farther than city limits,
But she squared her shoulders, and thought of
how her mama told her
To keep the faith, fight the fight, and run the
Race

~ One ~

"Every time I go for a run and reach the end, I feel a great sense of accomplishment. I love celebrating every little victory."
~Nadine, runner for fourteen years

"Set your soles on fire. Blaze ahead at full speed. Keep your faith alive, as you're running to your dreeeeeams!"

I belted out the chorus of my favorite Drake Douglas tune louder than the car radio. Those speakers couldn't keep up with my pipes. In my driver's seat, I was the star.

I imagined standing on a stage in front of an adoring audience, lit by a spotlight. I'd have my hair teased to high-heaven, and obviously, I'd wear a royal blue floor-length gown with plenty of sequins. When the applause brought me back on stage for several encores, I'd blow kisses to my adoring fans.

A horn cut through the banjo-laced country music, and I snapped back to reality. The spotlight dissolved into a green traffic light, and the adoring fans became a line of annoyed cars waiting for me to go instead of chanting for me to stay. One of them honked a second time.

"Sorry," I said, with a quick smile and a wave. I pulled into the grocery store parking lot, my cheeks now burning with embarrassment.

Maybe I should consider a career change? I thought. If I were a singer, instead of a kindergarten teaching assistant, I could have someone else drive

11

me around. Not to mention I'd actually make enough money to put Amelia through college.

I sat back in my seat for a moment and thought about traveling in a huge RV, complete with my own chauffeur, plush leather reclining chairs, and an endless supply of sweet tea with a touch of lemon.

My phone rang, jarring me out of my new relaxing scenario.

"Hi, Amelia." I balanced the phone between my ear and shoulder and turned the music down. Drake Douglas's song continued to play softly, and I tapped my foot to the beat.

"Mom, where are you?"

"Store. I'll be home soon." I fumbled around for my purse.

"What's for dinner?"

"It's a surprise."

I had the evening planned perfectly. I would make Amelia's favorite dish, and we would eat on our little back porch just as the spectacular Kentucky sunset lit the sky pink and purple. A robin, perched on a nearby tree, would chirp a lovely tune.

I had to create as many of these moments as possible, before she left for college in the fall.

Amelia suddenly faded from my vision of the perfect evening, and I could see my new future: I would sit alone on the porch and scarf down a half-frozen pizza. A crow would screech, and it would start to rain.

I suddenly felt sick and pushed the thought from my mind. Tonight would be perfect. No crows, no rain, and absolutely no frozen pizzas. Just a sunset, and Amelia's favorite – chicken 'n dumplin's.

"Mom. Momma."

I snapped back to reality. "Sorry, Ameils. Zoned

out for a second."

"It's fine, I'm used to it." Amelia laughed. "What were you picturing this time?"

"What if I quit my job at the school and become a country singer? Imagine riding around in an RV with our own driver and traveling all around the states." I decided not to worry her with the frozen pizza vision.

"Mom, you can't remember words to any songs. You thought Shania Twain sang, 'the best thing about being a woman is the prerogative to have a little brunch.'"

"It is," I said defensively.

"Besides," Amelia continued, "I thought you were going to finish your certification and become a teacher. Isn't that your dream?"

"Brunch is a better option. You and I both know it. Besides, it's my prerogative to have a little dream," I sang.

"Nice deflection," Amelia said, and I could practically see her rolling her eyes.

"It's a skill. I'll be home right after I get groceries. Bye, sweetie," I said, but Amelia had already hung up.

My thoughts jumped back to my life after Amelia left for college.

Maybe I wouldn't eat frozen pizzas nightly, but I would certainly bawl my eyes out, go through a million boxes of tissues, and sit home all by myself. Amelia would probably never call, never visit home again, and go off to travel the world. People would take one look at me and say, "your daughter is so talented. She must get that from her father."

Of course, I'd be happy for my little girl, but I would have to adopt about twenty dogs to get over my lack of accomplishment and empty-nest depression.

A peppy radio DJ interrupted my train of thought.

"You're listening to 101.5, The Boot. That was *Running to your Dreams* by the hottest new country star, Drake Douglas. Now, if you're a Douglas fan, you're gonna want to hear this. We're giving away an early Christmas present to four lucky winners. It's a VIP dream day with Drake himself. You heard right. You and three guests could win an entire day with Drake Douglas. All you have to do is grab your phone and text 37326, or DREAM, to 101.5 the Boot. The thirteenth text wins the prize. That's DREAM 37326. Don't miss out on this dream."

I stared at the radio, the words hitting me like a monster truck at the Kentucky State Fair.

A dream day with Drake Douglas? Did I hear correctly? I love Drake Douglas. I love his music.

I imagined a huge box under my Christmas tree with a golden ribbon. I would lift the lid to find Drake Douglas inside. Not only did he have the voice of an angel, he wasn't bad on the eyes, either.

I walked to the grocery store entrance in a daze, thinking about Drake Douglas and his dreamy voice.

Why not give it a shot? It's my prerogative to have a little dream, isn't it?

I hit 'New Message' on my phone, punched 3-7-3-2-6, filled in the number of the station, and hit "Send." Nothing happened.

Laughing at myself, I stuffed my phone in my back pocket and grabbed a shopping basket. What was I doing entering a radio contest? Some dreams weren't meant to be. Like me with my hair teased up and body poured into a sequined dress.

Ridiculous.

At least the radio idea had my heart beating faster than it would be on a normal trip down the meat aisle.

My phone buzzed in my pocket, and I answered it while eyeing a package of chicken.

"This is Kelly Jo."

"Hello, Kelly Jo. You are the lucky thirteenth person to text station 101.5 for a dream day with Drake Douglas. Please hold for details."

I dropped my phone in shock, and it clattered to the grocery store floor. *I won? No way.*

Surely this was some silly prankster, and I had to buy something or pay for something. Or worse, they'd put me on the radio live and I'd have to guess an answer to some stupid trivia question. Though honestly, I'd probably get it right if it were about Drake Douglas.

I scrambled to pick up my phone just as a peppy man chirped over the line.

"Hello, Kelly Jo. Thank you for waiting. You are our lucky thirteenth listener to text."

"I've never won anything. Ever," I said. "I'm more of a loser. I lose at guys. Finishing college. My job. The only thing I can't lose is weight."

The butcher at the meat counter paused midway through slicing a block of cheese and shot me an amused look.

"Sorry," I said into the phone, and turned my back to the butcher. "Ignore all that."

"Will do," the man said, still upbeat.

"So, this isn't a joke. I won. I actually won?" My heart pounded faster, and my voice became louder by the second. "I won the dream day with Drake Douglas?"

"Yes ma'am."

"Thank you, Jesus!"

"Ma'am, can I help you?" The butcher interrupted.

I whirled around to face him, shook my head frantically, and put my finger to my lips. He fell silent. The teacher look worked every time.

"What's your full name?" The man on the phone said, his exuberance matching mine.

"Kelly. Kelly Jo Raymond. Age thirty-nine and holding, just like the song, only I actually am thirty-nine." I pressed the phone closer to my mouth and lowered my voice. "My address is 382 Henry Drive, Nicholasville, Kentucky. I have one daughter. I am a teacher's assistant at Rose Will Elementary School. I've been a teacher's assistant for almost seventeen years. I want to be a full-time teacher, but I didn't finish my degree yet. But I'm close."

"Um, only your name is fine for now, Mrs. Kelly Jo Raymond."

"It's Miss," I answered automatically. My palms were sweaty, and I readjusted my grip on the phone. I had actually won. I glanced at the butcher and announced, "I. Won. Can you believe it? I won."

"Congrats... Um, I'll be in the back if you need me," he whispered.

"Gotcha. *Miss* Kelly Jo Raymond," the chirpy man on the other end of the line said, his voice never losing its sunny quality. "Let me go over some of the logistics. First, to claim the prize, you'll need a signed note from your medical doctor stating you are fit to run the Jingle Bell 5K Run on December sixteenth. You and three guests will all need medical clearance. You can only run the race if at least three of you can run, and you'll need—"

16

"Run? Wait, what? Run a what?" My stomach lurched. No one had said anything about running. They talked about presents and magical times with Drake Douglas and opening a beautifully wrapped gift to find him inside, ready to personally serenade me. Okay, maybe I added the last part.

"Drake will be running the Jingle Bell Run with you and three of your guests, like we announced on the radio. The race benefits music programs in Kentucky schools. Now, let me get a little more—"

"Wait a minute, pumpkin. I won a contest to run a 5K?" My lucky break was quickly turning into a nightmare.

"Yes. Along with four front-row tickets to Drake's evening Christmas concert after the run that day." The announcer still tried to sound perky and excited, but I could hear a slight shift in his voice.

He could be annoyed all he wanted, but I needed answers. I paused, took a deep breath, and then slowly exhaled. It was something I always told my kindergartners to do when they were upset.

"Ma'am? Are you still there?"

"I thought this was a *prize*," I said. "Four tickets to a dream day with Drake Douglas."

"Yes ma'am." The announcer sounded fully agitated now, all the peppiness drained from his voice.

"I couldn't run down my driveway if my life depended on it," I said, now near panic.

"No worries," the announcer said, his voice dripping with false empathy. "It's only a 5K, and you have plenty of time to train for it. Come down to our Lexington office by next Friday with a medical release from your doctor to pick up your tickets." His voice abruptly went back to its peppy

17

broadcaster mode. "Congratulations, Miss Kelly Jo Raymond. Hope to see you by next Friday."

I stared at my cell phone. My mind a blank. No lyrics, no grocery list, no daydreams. I finally shoved the cell phone into my hip pocket and walked through the grocery store in a daze. I grabbed a brownie mix, paid, and left.

~ Two ~

"Don't be intimidated by other runners. Just get up, dress up, and show up!"
-Cindy, runner for forty-one years

Double chocolate Godiva brownie mix and receipt in hand, I walked to my pickup in a daze. *Could I really do it? Me?*

Exercise was not my strong suit. Last year at the start of school I tried Zumba. I hated it. Before that, I tried yoga, bikes at the gym, and swimming at the YMCA. I hated it all. How in the name of Heaven and all that is good could I run a 5K? And with an angel like Drake Douglas at my side?

I imagined running with Drake. A strand of my hair would fall into my eyes and he would gently brush it away.

"You have eyes like the Kentucky sky on a summer's day," he'd declare. Then he'd go on about how I was so interesting, smart, and athletic. And he wouldn't call my legs sturdy like my mother always did. He'd tell me that my legs looked like Carrie Underwoods'.

My cheeks burned when I imagined what would actually happen—me wearing unflattering athletic shorts while sweat poured down my face despite the freezing cold December weather. I would pass out in a mound of gray snow just after crossing the start line. Drake Douglas would witness the whole thing.

I couldn't run a stupid race. I tossed the brownie mix on the passenger seat next to a faded recipe

19

card for my grandmother's chicken 'n dumplin's.

"Oh, for Heaven's sake," I said. "I forgot the dang chicken."

I returned to the entrance of the grocery store to get a shopping buggy. Might as well get groceries for the week, while I was spending a million years here lost in my thoughts, or I'd have nothing but brownie mix to last the week.

I grabbed the handle of the buggy and jerked, nothing happened. I yanked again. Still nothing. The stupid buggy was jammed into the row of endless carts corralled in the entrance. Of course, it was stuck. Story of my life. I sighed and moved to the next cart over. It wouldn't budge.

Maybe running will somehow help me with my grocery shopping, I thought drily.

I moved to the last buggy and pulled with full force. It came free immediately, and I lost my balance. I tried to catch myself but in my little scuffle-square-dance, I tripped over my own Fit and one of my worn blue flats flew off my foot and over the carts.

So much for this being my lucky day. I won a prize to *exercise*, and now I was shoeless, sitting on my rear. I was practically Cinderella.

I hopped on one foot toward my flat but after two hops, I froze, balancing on one sturdy leg. There, standing in front of me, was a woman dressed in a pressed gray suit and silk scarf patterned with Jack-O-Lanterns. Her lips curled into a smirk, and with horror I realized she had seen the entire scuffle. Even the stepsisters hadn't witnessed Cinderella's transformation back into a country bumpkin at midnight. Lucky Cinderella. Me, on the other hand? Of course, I had a witness, and of course it was my sorority big sister from the University of

Kentucky, Monica. Trying to pull myself together, I tucked wisps of brown hair behind my ears. I was a hot mess.

"Monica, hi." I tried to gracefully touch my bare toe to the cement without Monica noticing my shoeless foot.

Monica towered over my short frame, especially in her high-heeled pumps. She stared down her straight nose at me, a smirk still edged across her lips.

"Kelly Jo, it's been months. I haven't seen you since the girls' last a cappella concert in the spring."

I nodded and smiled automatically, but my heart raced. Sure, I remembered that concert. That was one of the many nights I'd like to erase from my brain. Permanently.

Just before the show, Monica told Amelia's a cappella group that they had to change their formation.

"Some performers need to be in the back, so they wouldn't block the others from being heard," she said, and then she moved *only* Amelia. Monica claimed it was about musical blocking, not physical blocking, but Amelia was so upset she locked herself in her room for the entire weekend.

"I'm fat, ugly, and I can't sing," she cried from behind her door.

I tried to comfort my sweet little girl, but the whole incident left me burning with anger. How could Monica have been so cruel to Amelia?

I determined that Monica did it because she hated me, but I was still shocked that she would stoop that low.

Monica and I were best friends once, back in college. She was my sorority "big sister," and I adored her. I was even a bridesmaid in her wedding.

She married her college sweetheart, Michael, and I thought they were the perfect couple. At their wedding I met Jake, her husband's best friend. Jake and I fell madly in love, but within a few short months I went from madly in love to desperately alone, because I had become "Jake's mistake." At least, that's what Monica told me.

Apparently, Monica couldn't understand why I would drop Jake and leave college to have a baby. She said I should stay in school. She was a couple of years older and was also expecting. I thought we could support each other, but instead, our friendship disintegrated because she did things the "right way" and I didn't.

It could have been so amazing, both of our girls growing up together. It was not the story I had written for my life. I thought Jake was my Prince Charming, but he turned out to be the villain. And so, apparently, was Monica. She was the witch out to get me and my little girl, too.

"You seem flustered. Are you all right, Kelly Jo?" Monica's loud, brassy voice snapped me out of the flashback.

Trying to ignore the hotness of my cheeks, I said, "I'm great, in fact. How are you? How are your music classes at the high school going?" My voice dripped with fake interest.

"Amazing. Thank you so much for asking." She paused for a second. She sounded like her old self, but then her voice became harsh again. "Tryouts were wonderful. I think this year is going to be my best set of talent yet. Not only are my new freshmen talented, the seniors are wonderful in my select choir, too. Especially Amelia. She keeps improving by the week. I'm so proud of her. Students like her make teaching so rewarding."

I bit my lip in annoyance. Monica had no right declaring how she was proud of *my* Amelia.

"Lindsay has this new vocal coach from the University of Kentucky who is working with her two times a week," Monica continued, not noticing my irritated silence. "She said Lindsay definitely will be able to pursue anything she wants with music. Lindsay also got an audition at the Blair School of Music in Nashville. She's also looking at Juilliard and the Boston Conservatory. I'm sure she'll have her choice of scholarships."

Auditions? Scholarships? Oh, my Heavens! I hadn't even thought about auditions or scholarships for Amelia. The race was on and I was already way behind.

"Have you planned on any college visits yet for Amelia?" Monica asked, and this time I felt she could read my panicked expression. "Applications are due by January first, and Lindsay is almost done. I hired a career coach to provide some assistance for her. Maybe you could do the same for Amelia?"

"Maybe," I said noncommittally. I didn't need advice from Monica on how to help my daughter.

"If you want her number, just let me know." Monica cleared her voice and continued. "Are you planning on attending the first booster club meeting next week for the a cappella group? We're in desperate need of new dresses in various sizes. Do you think you'll have time? You're always a great help, Kells."

I couldn't talk with Monica right now. Not about Amelia, dresses, college, or parent booster clubs. I had to get away before I exploded in annoyance.

23

I stood up straight and stretched out my foot surreptitiously, trying to reach my blue flat with one toe so I could make my getaway. Where was my fairy godmother when I needed her?

"Sure. Yup. Time. I'll be at the meeting." I wasn't making any sense, but I didn't care. I would say anything if it meant escaping this conversation.

"Are you still working part-time with the kindergarteners at Rose Will Elementary?"

I was pretty sure she said the words "part-time" in slow motion, voice dripping with judgment.

"Or did you finally get your certification to teach full time? I know you've been talking about that for years." Monica leaned forward and her sheet of thick, dark hair fell over her shoulders in an annoyingly perfect way.

Usually, I loved autumn but at this moment, I wanted to fast-forward and find myself by a fireside with a mug of hot chocolate, all spooky visions of Monica banished by Christmas cheer and Drake Douglas.

"Yes, Drake Douglas," I murmured.

"Pardon me?" Monica asked.

"I'm so, so busy working," I said quickly. "I'm just a busy lil bumble bee."

She didn't need to know that I hadn't completed my certification. When I left school to have Amelia, Monica had said that I would never finish my certification if I didn't do it back then.

I didn't want to give her the satisfaction of being right, even though she was. I felt too old to go back for the sixteen hours of student teaching plus the one semester of classes I still needed. It was too expensive. I had Amelia to think about—and now the Jingle Bell Run.

I reached down, slid on my shoe, and smiled at Monica.

"It turns out that I'm not only working at Rose Will Elementary, taking care of Amelia all by myself, but I'm actually running," I said, the words falling out of my mouth and floating away before I could catch them. "That's my new passion. Running to my dreams. I'm even running the Jingle Bell 5k this December with Drake Douglas."

My dear God in Heaven, had I really said that? I stepped back a bit, surprised by my own announcement, but I felt an unexpected flash of confidence from the words.

"I don't see you as the running type," Monica said, obviously thrown by my declaration. "I thought you hated exercise."

Her eyes lingered on my silver-studded jeans, like she could see through to my sturdy legs with X-ray vision.

"You thought wrong," I said. "I adore it."

"I'm surprised," she said.

You and me both.

"Good luck with the race," she continued, still with a note of surprise in her voice. "I'll see you at our first mandatory parent booster meeting next week." Monica swiveled on her gray pumps and poof! she was gone.

I stood in the entrance of the grocery store. The air-conditioned blast from inside hit me, and I felt the flash of confidence drift away, replaced by dread.

I knew nothing about running half a mile, much less an entire 5k. I literally didn't even know how many miles were in a 5k. And now I had announced to the biggest gossip frenemy in town that I'd be

25

competing in a race.

I needed to talk with Fiona, Shruti, and Georgia, immediately. I grabbed my phone and sent a group text: *"Y'all will NEVER believe what just happen-ed."*

I pinched my arm, but there was apparently no waking up from the nightmare.

~ Three ~

"For our training, we ran from one telephone pole to another, then walked. Then we extended the running to two poles, three, etc., until we were running most of the time."
-Melissa, runner for fourteen years

"Mom, how in the world will you work at Rose Will this fall, take me to college visits, and train for a 5K?" Amelia asked while I ladled chicken 'n dumplin's into her bowl.

"I'm Super Mom," I joked. "I have a stretchy suit in my closet. I wear it only when needed."

"You're so weird." Amelia glanced at me with a hint of a smile. She stirred her bowl but didn't take a bite. Finally, she said in a faux casual voice, "Hey, maybe I should wait a year before I go to college. I could do something really awesome instead, like go to Nashville to sing."

She looked at me anxiously with her big, blue eyes framed with long lashes. She got those eyes from me, but she got her musical talent from her dad. At least she got one good thing from him.

"Not this again, sweetheart," I said, waving a hand dismissively. "Get your education first. Then you can follow your dreams."

"I've wanted to talk with you about this, Momma." Amelia pressed on. "Maybe I could take a gap year and sing."

"You don't have to take a gap year for that. You can sing at college."

27

Amelia slumped in her chair. "That's not what I meant."

She fell silent and I wracked my brain to think of something to restart the conversation. This was the most talkative Amelia had been in days, other than talking about food, and I didn't want it to stop.

All summer she had worked at the mall during the day and then shut herself in her room and blasted angsty pop music all night. After school started, she spent all her time in class, ate dinner, and then back to her room again with the music. I had to take every minute I could get.

"Do you think they'd let me do the 5K on roller skates?" I joked again, trying not to lose my window. "Or how about your old Razor™ scooter?"

Amelia stared at me for a moment, and then cracked a smile. "You're running the race in December, Mom. I think you'll probably need snow-shoes."

"Ice skates?" I asked.

"And a couple of layers of long underwear," Amelia said. "Actually, how are you going to do this 5K? You don't exercise—ever."

"Yes, I do," I said, slightly annoyed. "I run errands. Like taking out the garbage. Sometimes, I walk Fiona's dog around the block when she's out of town visiting her parents. I walk all around the hallways taking my little kiddos to their specials. I do lots of exercise stuff."

"Are you serious?" Amelia's blue eyes sparkled like little stars, and she laughed. This was how I wished things always were. The two of us, like old times, cracking up and hanging out together.

"You bet your lil' booty. Speaking of booty, imagine how great mine will look when I'm done

28

training." I rose up out of my chair and shook my rear.

"Momma, you are so weird." Amelia giggled.

I twirled around shaking my rear and plopped back in my chair.

"But what about your work? You said you might spend the fall applying for classes so you can finish your certification next year while I'm at college. If you're training and exercising, you won't have time."

"I'll git'er-done." I punched my fist in front of my chest and added, "Sometime or another."

Even as I said the words, I didn't really believe them. The truth was, I didn't even know where to start with any of it.

"No offense," Amelia said.

Oh boy, here it comes, I thought. *Nothing good ever follows that intro.*

"You really haven't done anything interesting recently," Amelia continued. "You always talk about it or imagine it. I mean, you take care of me and work part-time and stuff, but that's it."

A wave of sadness washed over me. Was that how she viewed me, as a person who could only dream and never actually do anything?

"I guess that's about to change," I said, more firmly than I felt, and Amelia nodded.

"I guess it is."

I shook off my internal pity party. Amelia and I were actually having a conversation and laughing. This was a magical night, and believe it or not, it was all due to Monica. I chuckled at the thought.

"What are you laughing about, Momma?"

"Just thinking about how funny it is that I won a prize to run."

Maybe Monica was my fairy godmother. After all, she was the one who pushed me into saying I was going to run. *But was I? Could I?*

"Maybe this is a sign."

"A sign for what, baby?"

Amelia took a deep breath and whispered, "That I shouldn't go to college next year."

"Heavens to Betsy," I said, irritated. "How does my running this race have anything to do with you going to college?"

"Mom just listen for once." *Great. I was back to Mom, instead of Momma.* "I don't know what I want to do for my career, but I know I want to take a year off and maybe move to Nashville. I want to do something that I want to do, not what everyone else thinks I should do. I could waitress during the day and sing at night."

She was suddenly more animated than I had seen her in weeks. She sat up straight in her chair, eyes bright from something other than one of my silly jokes. "I talked with Monica about it after practice the other day. She said she had some ideas."

"Wait, who? Monica? What? Why on earth would you talk to *her*?"

"She had some gap year ideas she said she wants to talk to me about. That means we don't need to visit colleges. You'll have time to train and fill out your college applications. It's a win-win situation. Isn't that what you always say?" She twirled her spoon faster in her bowl of dumplings.

"Amelia Sue, what on earth?" What was Monica doing sticking her nose into my daughter's business? The evil villain was messing with my happily ever after.

"I'm serious, Mom. I don't want to go to

30

college." Amelia folded her arms.

"You'll feel more excited when you visit some colleges." I smiled at Amelia, hoping to get back our moment. "You just need to—"

Good Girl by Carrie Underwood interrupted me.

"Hold on just a second," I said, grabbing my phone, "that's your grandma's ringtone." I held the phone up to my ear. "Hey, Mom. Is everything all right?"

"Hi, honey." My mom's voice suddenly filled me with a weird mixture of calm and edginess. "You left a message. What was it you wanted to tell me?"

"It's nothing." I looked at Amelia. "I wanted to tell you I won this contest today."

"Did you win a scholarship for college? For Amelia? For you?" Her voice sounded demanding and too loud in my ear. So much for the calm.

"No Mom, you know those lil' contests on the radio on 101.5 the Boot?" I stood and paced the kitchen. "I entered and I actually won."

Amelia's chair scraped on the floor, and I turned toward the table. She stood and cleared the table. I put a hand on the receiver.

"Wait, Amelia, let's work this out. Let's talk a little more. Just wait one second."

"What?" My mom cut in. "Is Amelia all right? What do you need to work out?"

"Mom, everything is fine," I said, already exasperated. "We were just having dinner and talking about college visits."

"*You* were talking about college visits," Amelia muttered. She scraped the rest of her dumplings into the garbage.

"You're finally going back to college? Good for you." My mom nearly blew out my eardrum.

31

"No, Mom, for Amelia. She's a senior, remember?"

"I know she's a senior. I'm not senile. At least not yet. So, what is this contest thing anyway? What did you win?" Mom continued, obviously not hearing my dinner explanation.

My eyes remained focused on every move Amelia made. "It's a 5K Christmas benefit run with Drake Douglas and then a – "

"*Drake Douglas?*"

"Yeah, a 5K benefit run with him and then front row seats at the following concert. Amelia, wait—"

"A run? Kelly Jo, are you daydreaming again?" My Mom interrupted. "I thought you said you were going to run. Bless your heart, you can't walk past your mailbox, much less run a 5K."

"Thanks for the confidence, Mom." I tried to stay calm. "I may not do it anyway, I just thought it was fun, and wanted to tell you. That's all."

Amelia poured a bit more of my homemade sweet tea into her mason jar glass. It was the start of her nightly routine. She would take her tea up to her room, lock the door, and blast music until she drifted off to sleep.

"I gotta go, Mom. Finishing up dinner. Love you," I said quickly, hoping to end the conversation before my mother started listing my other shortcomings. If she started on that, I'd be on the phone for the next month.

I hung up and turned back to Amelia. "Honey, wait."

Amelia looked at me, her eyes expectant. I stood there trying to think, but my mind was weirdly blank. Amelia's shoulders slumped.

"I think I have homework or something." She left

the kitchen, and all I saw was the swish of her ponytail disappearing behind her bedroom door at the top of the stairs.

Once again, my opportunity to make things right was lost. I walked back to the table, plopped down in my chair, and shoved the last bite of dumplings into my mouth. Of course, they were cold.

~ Four ~

"When you first start running, find friends to run with—that always makes the time pass quickly, and friends are great motivators."
-Tricia, runner for twenty-five years

I flung open the thick door to Main and Maple, and the scent of rich coffee washed over me. I inhaled deeply, and instantly felt a rush of excitement.

I loved our monthly coffee meetings, and I couldn't wait to tell my best friends Fiona, Georgia, and Shruti about the "Dream Day" contest.

Fiona and I worked together at the school. She was the put together teacher, hair smoothed back in a blonde ponytail and skinny jeans tucked into black riding boots, every single day. I was her crazy sidekick teacher's aide with my teased brunette hairdo full of so much hairspray that I couldn't stand too close to candles, and rhinestones on every item of clothing I owned. We were the perfect duo.

Georgia and I met at church. She sang hymns in a booming voice and clicked instantly. She had bright red hair, freckles, and a voluptuous figure, and made a perfect addition to our friend group, with her tell-it-like-it-is sass.

Shruti was my most recent friend. We met in line at a sample sale and bonded together to get a great deal on winter coats. I even convinced her to get one with fur trim, even though she insisted that the purple faux fur "wasn't practical." She had a dark complexion, a fit frame, and wore simple neutral tones. Quiet and patient, she rounded out the group perfectly.

I spotted the three women perched in brown leather chairs in our usual back corner of the cozy café.

"Hey ladies." I waved.

When I lifted my arm into the air, I collided with a man—a gorgeous, broad-shouldered, disheveled brown-haired man. He wore a white, finely starched shirt. For a brief moment, our eyes met, and my heart fluttered. *Total Prince Charming material*, I thought dreamily.

And then I knocked into his cup, and coffee splattered all over his white shirt.

"Oh, bless your heart. I am so, so very sorry." I clapped my hands over my mouth and assessed the damage.

The coffee dripped down his shirt in slow motion, pooling on his fine leather belt. My eyes lingered on his broad, muscular chest. *Oh, yeah. Definitely Prince Charming material.*

I wrenched open my purse and dug through it, past a lengthy to-do list, a newly purchased book of colleges filled with Post-It Notes, receipts, and a melted chocolate bar. Finally, I unearthed a tissue and offered it to him.

When he reached to take it, I brushed his rough, warm hand, and I resisted the urge to interlace my fingers with his.

"I really am sorry," I said again, my voice a high-pitched squeak. When I glanced down at the tissue, I realized it was covered in Passion Pink ChapStick™.

"I didn't like this shirt anyway," he said with a lopsided grin. His teeth were brilliantly white and

35

perfectly straight. He was Prince Charming *and* a Crest™ commercial, all in one. "It's kind of stuffy."

"Still, you have to wear a shirt. You can't just walk around bare chested," I rambled. "That would stop traffic. Because everyone would rubberneck to look. I mean, I don't know what I mean." My cheeks instantly flushed. What was I *saying*?

"The drivers of Kentucky are safe," he said, chuckling. "I have another shirt in my truck."

"That's swell," I said. "The cat's pajamas." *The cat's pajamas? Way to sound like a ninety-year-old grandma, Kelly Jo.*

"It was truly a pleasure colliding with you," he said, winked, and then disappeared out the door.

For a few heavenly seconds I remained frozen, staring out the door at this mystery man, my hand still in the air holding the tissue.

Wait a second. I thought. *I know him.*

"But *how* do I know him?" I mumbled against the glass.

It suddenly hit me—high school youth group. No wonder I hadn't been able to place him right away. It had been a hot second since I'd been in high school, and he had certainly grown up. Wow, had he grown up.

I watched him across the parking lot and imagined hopping into his passenger seat, turning the radio to a country song, putting my Fit on the dash and saying, "Let's go for a drive, cowboy."

I had lost my mind. I needed to get a life. A *real* life. I turned and realized that everyone in the coffee shop was staring at me.

"It's totally fine," I said. "He has an extra shirt in his truck."

The conversation in the shop resumed, and I

quickly wove through a maze of chairs to my friends.

"Bet you didn't realize this coffee shop now provides entertainment to go with your espresso," I said, dropping into a curtsy and slumping into a seat on the couch next to Fiona, Georgia, and Shruti. All three of them shook with laughter.

"We've all been there, sugar," Georgia said, waving a hand dismissively. "You picked the cutest guy in town to bump into. I'm sure you had an amazing daydream going on the entire time."

"You bet your britches I did."

"Speaking of britches, that's quite a trick to get him out of his," Fiona teased.

"I spilled it on his shirt, not his jeans." I said over their renewed laughter.

I looked around the table, which was crowded with lipstick-rimmed coffee cups. "Oh no," I said, "are y'all done with your coffee already?"

"Of course not. We were waiting for you." Shruti tucked a section of thick, wavy black hair behind one ear. Always serious.

"And we'll always excuse tardiness if it gets you a meet and greet with a gorgeous guy like Mr. Sexy Southerner." Georgia sipped her coffee with a pinky in the air. "Did you manage to catch his name during the one-person male wet t-shirt contest?"

"No, but I think I actually know him from a long time ago. He went to my youth group, back in the day. Erik something. Erik... Wellsworth." I thought of his chocolate-brown eyes and melted inside like a gooey marshmallow on a s'more. Boy, did I want some more!

"Where was he when I walked into the cafe this morning? I would have bumped into that construction—calendar boy in a heartbeat," Fiona said, raising a brow and toying with a small diamond stud in her ear. Yeah, right. She would never run into anyone. She was too classy and put together. I was the hot mess.

I started to relax for the first time all morning, feeling the warm glow I felt when I was around my friends.

"Honey, did you finally schedule your college visit to Vanderbilt for Amelia?" Georgia scooted her chair closer to me and crossed her curvy legs.

"Yeah, it looks amazing in the pictures. Have y'all ever been to Nashville?" I asked.

Georgia raised her hand. "Sweetie, I know Vandy. Very prestigious university. My pediatrician graduated from Vanderbilt, top of her class. She told me when I interviewed her."

Of course, Georgia interviewed her pediatrician, and of course she was the best. Ever since Georgia adopted her daughter, Grace, she injected every conversation with mommy details. I didn't mind. I was like that when I first had Amelia.

"She's acting so weird about college," I said, and sank further into the leather couch. "She claims she doesn't want to go. I thought maybe with Nashville being big on music, she'd at least consider going to Vanderbilt."

"What is it, Kells?" Fiona asked. "You seem discouraged."

"She's leaving in less than one year, and I'm not ready. We hardly talk, and when we do, she rambles about not going to college. Where is that all coming from?" I sounded like a guitar out of tune. "What am I going to do?"

"Honey, I'm not ready, either," Georgia said. She set the mug down with a little too much force and a bit of coffee spilled out of the cup. "Just thinking about my baby girl leaving makes me bawl my eyes out. I love having Gracie around so much, I could talk with her forever and for always."

"Gracie is in *kindergarten*," Fiona said, shaking her head. She opened the drawstring on her leather backpack purse and pulled out a moist toilette, using it to mop up the mess on the table.

"I know," Georgia said, her eyes starting to well up. "It seems like just yesterday we were bringing her home from China. She was so tiny. Now she's practically grown up. The day I dropped her off at kindergarten, she said, 'it's okay, mommy, I can do this by myself.'"

Georgia leaned back to stop tears from blurring her thick mascara. On cue, Fiona handed her a tissue and Georgia dabbed at her eyes.

"You're always reminding us to rejoice and be anxious about nothing," Fiona said to Georgia. "Let's rejoice about Gracie being in kindergarten, and that she loves it. You've got more than a few years before she heads off to college."

Georgia blew her nose and smiled.

"Kelly Jo, it's going to be all right with Amelia, too," Fiona continued. "She'll come around. You're a great mom."

"Will it?" I sighed. "Am I?"

Shruti placed a hand on my arm. She had an intricate henna tattoo snaking up to her forearm, which I thought must be practice for Diwali, the Hindu Festival of Lights coming up soon.

"Ladies," she said softly, "Kelly Jo hasn't had a coffee yet. We can't solve all of life's problems until she has at least one cup. What would you like, Kelly? It's on me today."

"Shruti, you don't have to," I said starting to stand, but she gently guided me back into the chair.

"I know, but I'd love to. I'll be right back." She slipped over to the counter.

"Hope she picks something better than this sugarless mixture. Whatever I'm drinking tastes awful," Georgia grumbled, looking down at her mug, and I raised a brow.

"Why are you drinking it, then?"

"I'm on a new diet. It's a thirty-day detox. I have no idea how I'm going to make it without Halloween candy, Thanksgiving pumpkin pie, and Christmas cookies. My heavens, I love my Christmas cookies. And what will I bake with Gracie? Baked carrot cookies?" Georgia sipped her coffee through pinched lips. "My doctor also recommended exercise. It's a load of hooey if you ask me. I don't have time to exercise. Gracie is only at kindergarten for three hours, and that's shopping or coffee time."

If Georgia's doctor said *she* needed exercise, I could only imagine what he would tell *me*.

"Bless your heart, honey, you are a lost cause." I *imagined a man in a lab coat with a disapproving expression. "Here's a diet boot camp I think you should consider attending."* I'd be shipped off before I could even say *sugar*.

"I could use more exercise this fall," Fiona said thoughtfully. Georgia caught my eye and stifled a smile. Fiona was in perfect shape. She didn't have half the sweet tooth that Georgia and I did.

"Hon, you look like Meghan Markle's long-lost twin. Polished and perfect," Georgia said sternly.

"I sit at a desk all day. When I was younger, I used to ride horses all the time. I miss being outside and getting all that fresh air and a great work out."

40

"Fi, what are you talking about? You're on your Fit with the kiddos all day," I said.

"True," she relented. "However, I have an ulterior motive for wanting to exercise *outside* the classroom."

"What?" I said, knitting my brows together.

She adjusted her already perfect ponytail. "The chances of running into an attractive man are significantly higher," she said, with a telling glance toward the spot I had collided with Erik.

"Here's your pumpkin-spiced latte, my friend." Shruti handed me a warm coffee mug.

I closed my eyes and inhaled the sweet pumpkin aroma. When I opened them, a picture on the mug caught my attention. It was a stick figure of a girl running into a coffee shop. Bold letters on the side of the mug spelled out, "Running on Empty?"

I nearly dropped the mug. "I do declare."

"Is it too hot?" Shruti asked, concerned.

"No, it's perfect. In more ways than one. I almost forgot to tell you all some big news."

My excitement bubbling over, I forced myself to calm down enough to explain to them about the contest, the four tickets, medical releases, and that at least two people had to run with me at the Jingle Bell 5K with Drake Douglas. They stared at me, eyes wide.

"You won a ticket to see Drake Douglas and you didn't tell me immediately?" Fiona asked. "You know I love him."

Shruti leaned forward. "Are you sure this is legitimate, Kelly? People are always falling for scams. Did you give them any of your information? Credit card numbers? Social security number?"

Fiona raised her hand. "When is it? Where? Time?

I need details."

"I didn't just win one concert ticket. I won four—"

"You won more than one ticket?" Fiona threw her arms in the air like a charismatic woman in a worship service.

"I won four tickets to this crazy magical day with Drake. I'm supposed to participate in the Jingle Bell run, then go to the concert. There has to be at least three people running with him. For publicity. But I do have four tickets."

"There are three of us right here just waiting for you, Kelly Jo Raymond." Fiona pointed at each of us around the table. "Oh dear. I need a paper bag. This is the best news ever."

"Take a deep breath, Fi," I said. "I don't know if I can do it."

Fiona spit as she exhaled.

Georgia and Shruti both stared at me in disbelief.

"You're not makin' any sense, sweetie," Georgia said. "Don't you want to meet Dreamy Drake?"

"Yes, but I can't run," I said, feeling all my insecurities bubble to the surface. "I can barely walk to my mailbox."

"You don't have to run the race today," Shruti said sensibly. "I've read about all sorts of 'couch to 5k' training plans. You just do a little each day. Work up to your goal."

"I have to take Amelia on college visits. I don't have time to train."

"For Drake Douglas, you make time," Fiona insisted.

"If y'all haven't noticed, I don't actually complete things. I just dream," I said. "Exhibit A:

I've never finished my teaching certification. If I were a horse in the Kentucky Derby, they'd bet on me to come in dead last." I sighed, and my favorite bulky Kentucky-blue necklace bounced against my chest.

"You got that necklace last Black Friday, didn't you?" Fiona asked, pointing at it.

"It was a steal." I lifted my necklace off my chest and fingered the smooth stone.

"And wasn't that the day you bought those Hunter boots for Amelia at Macy's? You had to run to get the last pair of red ones. I'll never forget the look on that blonde woman's face when you beat her there. She was livid. Remember?" Fiona asked.

"Nobody was going to get in my way for those boots for Amelia. But what's your point, Fi?"

"If you put your mind to it, you can run. Maybe this race, this prize, is exactly the change you need." Fiona raised her mug. "I'm in."

"Wait, what?" I was confused.

Shruti grabbed her cell phone and pulled up her calendar app. "The race date is completely free. I'm in," she said.

Georgia, who had been uncharacteristically quiet, suddenly lifted her mug and announced, "If we're all doing this, I'm in, too. Why not?"

They all stared at me expectantly, and finally I raised my mug.

"Let's do this thang. To our first 5K!"

We clinked coffee mugs. At the noise, everyone in the coffee shop turned to stare yet again, but this time, I didn't care.

I was about to do something totally crazy, and it was totally for me. For us. I was Cinderella, making my own magic, and it was time to bring on the shoes.

~ Five ~

"I ran four times a week, working up to what I thought was a three-mile loop. I discovered the night before my 5K that I had miscalculated my distance and was really only running a two-mile loop. This was in the days before Garmin watches. I was absolutely panicked knowing I wasn't fully prepared to run the 5k!"
-Annette, runner for over twenty years

At six-thirty a.m., my alarm blared *Wide Open Spaces* by the Dixie Chicks. My mom hated it when I listened to them. "They're filling your head with sorghum. It's strong and sticky. Sounds and smells delicious, but just wait until you taste it," she said when I was a teenager.

My mother had a long list of things I did that she didn't approve of, and number one right now wasn't singing to the Dixie Chicks. It was the 5K. She thought I didn't have time and needed to focus on Amelia. She was also convinced I would blow out my knees and never be able to walk or work again.

I rolled over, smushed my face into my pillow, and closed my eyes, remembering her most recent lecture.

"I know about a girl who decided to run a 5k race," she said. "Her name was Laura-Beth, and she was exactly your age. She had sturdy legs like yours, but other than that, she was beautiful and talented. She practiced and trained, and on the day of the race, Laura-Beth was ready to go. The whistle

44

shrieked and the announcer yelled, 'Go!'

But then, before Laura-Beth could put one foot in front of the other, her heart stopped. She crumpled to the ground, and Laura-Beth never ran again. It turned out that after all that preparation and training, her poor heart just couldn't take it."

I imagined poor Laura-Beth, collapsed at the starting line—but slowly, the pavement at the race morphed into a stage, and the runners became an audience.

Amelia stood center-front in a beautiful black dress, alone in the spotlight. I tried to stand up to get closer, but the crowd pushed me back down, and she drifted away from me until she was a speck in the distance.

Bolting upright my eyes snapped open. Amelia wasn't singing, and I wasn't in the audience. I was in my bedroom and had drifted into some weird dream.

I drew in a deep breath. Maybe it was just a dream, but the truth was that Amelia *was* drifting away. She would leave for college, and that would be it.

Was I going to be like Laura-Beth? I pulled the covers over my head. Mom was right, I needed to focus, and spend time with Amelia. The whole running thing was just a crazy dream for someone else.

"Momma." I heard Amelia holler from downstairs. "Moooomma, are you coming?"

I sat straight up in bed and grabbed my alarm clock again, this time staring intently at the digits. Seven fifteen.

"I'm going to be late if we don't get going." Amelia walked into my room and perched on the edge of the bed with her backpack slung over one shoulder. "I can't believe you aren't ready."

"Don't get a bee all up in your bonnet. I'm coming," I said, still confused and half-asleep.

"Momma, you don't remember, do you? You're driving me to school today."

This brought me the rest of the way out of dream land. I tossed the covers and bolted upright. I had completely forgotten.

"You don't need me to take you." I grabbed a brush and raked it through my tousled hair. "You could ride the bus."

"Momma, do you really want me to hear the conversations that people on the bus have? Last week I heard the boy behind me talking about leaving an upper-decker in restaurant bathrooms."

"What in Heaven's name is an upper-decker?" I said, tossing my brush aside. "Actually, never mind. I don't want to know."

I threw on a sweatshirt over my pajamas and pulled on my favorite cowboy boots.

"Momma are you going like that?" Amelia crossed her arms over her pristine sweater and heart-shaped locket. Leave it to the fashionable teen to make me feel self-conscious about my wardrobe.

"Honey, since when do you care about what I wear to drive your little behind to school?" I looked around for my keys. We didn't have time for a *What Not to Wear* session this morning.

"It's the mandatory a cappella meeting this morning, before school, remember? All the parents are supposed to go. That's why you said you'd drive me."

"Oh, sugar! And I'm in this outfit?" I started undressing.

"Momma, we're going to be late," Amelia said, panicked. "Never mind about the outfit. Forget I said anything."

I ignored her and raced into the bathroom, swiping my toothbrush across my teeth and dumping open my makeup bag.

"I'm going to have to at least put something on my face." I grabbed a bottle of concealer and smudged it onto my under-eye circles. The bags under my eyes were dark, and my wrinkles seemed deeper than usual. I could use more than a little concealer, but I didn't have time.

"Mooomma, let's go!"

"Just pull up your big girl panties and hold on."

After a tense car ride, we speed-walked into the school auditorium and wrenched open the doors.

Light burst into the darkened room. Everyone turned and stared back at us. I followed Amelia into the closest open seats, halfway down an aisle. I slid past a prim mother and father, trying to ignore their judgmental glances at my sweatpants and cowboy boot ensemble.

"Sorry. Was that your toe?"

The woman glared at me. It was definitely her toe. I finally took my seat, cheeks flushed and crossed my arms.

Monica stood at the front of the auditorium, decked out in a gold poncho, a shiny necklace, and form-fitting slacks. She looked stunning.

"If I could have your attention back after that... interruption," Monica said, and cleared her throat. I ground my teeth. "The new singing group is really coming together. I'm so excited for my fourth wonderful year leading choir."

Blah, blah, blah, I thought. I fixed my gaze on her necklace. It looked like real diamonds.

Who gets to buy diamonds with a teacher's salary? I thought. *Her husband, Michael, must make big bucks at the bank.*

Or, I imagined, Monica had embezzled money. Michael had no idea. She would get caught and sent to prison, where I would visit her, decked out in a designer dress of my own. She would sit in her orange prison jumpsuit. Orange would be a terrible color for her. I smirked at the thought.

Monica's daughter, Lindsay, stepped up front to stand next to her mother.

Lindsay was the spitting image of Monica, only slightly shorter and with lighter hair. And, I noticed with surprise, with a quite different style of late. She had a green streak in her hair, and I even caught a glimpse of a nose ring.

I remembered when Monica and I went to get our belly buttons pierced before spring break my sophomore year and Monica's senior year at UK. We thought we were so edgy. We went and picked out extra teeny Kentucky blue bikinis to show off our new bling. Little did I know that silver adorable lil' bling would be coming off in less than two years. Pierced belly buttons and pregnancy go together like vinegar in your sweet tea.

When I realized I was pregnant, I ripped it out after I had an argument with Jake, who'd said he "wasn't ready" for that much responsibility. He walked out. I threw both my shoes at him, and then the belly-button ring, and he left for good. That was it for my college career. I never finished my senior year. And any bling was a distant blur.

Monica upgraded her bling for a diamond ring,

and she, like Jake, threw me to the side. She married Jake's best friend, Michael, my senior year, so it was clear where her loyalties were. She grabbed hold of Michael's arm and left me alone, and that was it for our so-called best friendship.

I didn't see her again until Amelia went to high school. We started to cross paths at events, but this time there was no friendship, no sisterhood, and no joint trips to the piercing parlor. Just tension and frustration.

I stared at Lindsay's nose ring, and fleetingly wished I knew her. She seemed like an interesting person. I knew she liked to sing, and Amelia told me she was a talented painter who had done all the backgrounds for the annual musical at the high school. When Amelia and Lindsay started to hang out, I thought maybe Monica and I could finally mend our fences after all these years, for the sake of our daughters' friendship. But then the whole dress thing blew up, so I put my white-picket fences back up and added an electric fence for protection.

"Um, Kelly Jo Raymond?"

Monica's sharp voice snapped me out of my thoughts.

"Are you still interested in helping raise money for the dresses for our Holiday Spectacular concert?" She looked at me expectantly.

People turned around to look in my direction and every single seat creaked, creating a cacophony of noise throughout the auditorium.

"Kelly Jo, is this still a fit for you? Being the costume coordinator?"

I stared up at her. *Is this still a* fit*? Was she trying to be funny, and reference what she had said to Amelia about the bigger girls standing in the back of the choir?*

49

"Would you mind heading up the committee this fall?" Monica asked again. Everyone stared at me, and I heard a couple of whispers at the front. One parent even pointed at my outfit.

"Uh, sure." I smiled and waved to everyone, especially the outfit pointer. Kill 'em with kindness.

"Thanks, Kelly Jo," Monica said, and cleared her throat. "Now, on to the next item of business. I have fliers with all of the important dates and details for the fall." She handed a stack of papers to kids in the choir, and they jumped off the stage and started handing them out to parents in the audience. "One very important date for y'all to note: our annual Holiday Spectacular concert will be on December sixteenth at eight o'clock in the evening. This is different than..."

She droned on. When the pile of papers finally got to me, I examined the schedule.

What? Holiday Spectacular

When? December 16th, 8-10 p.m.

I blinked, shook my head, and refocused on the paper. No way. This couldn't be right.

"Everyone loves this event. Freshman families, you're going to love this. Invite your grannies, grandpas—invite your postal worker," Monica said cheerily.

"Excuse me, Kelly Jo, could you pass over the rest of the fliers?" One of the moms sitting next to me held out a hand. I still clutched the entire pile of papers for the row, so I half-threw them in her direction.

"This is the event of the year to attend. All seniors are guaranteed solos. You won't want to miss this spectacular event." Monica clapped her annoyingly delicate hands.

I stood up and raised my not-delicate-at-all hand. "Excuse me," I said loudly. Once again, everyone stared back at me. "There must be a mistake. The Holiday Spectacular is always the first weekend in *November*. This schedule lists it in mid-December. I just wanted to make sure that everyone here knew about this mistake before—"

"There's no mistake, sweetie," Monica interrupted. "The December date was the best weekend for the concert—no football games or band events. There will also be construction work next door throughout the fall, and the company is going to use the high school lot to park trucks in the evening, so pushing the date later will help with any potential parking issues."

"We never have the Holiday Spectacular in December," I said stubbornly.

"In the past, that was true. But things change." She paused. "We've always had problems with this concert conflicting with other events. I really wanted to give our kids a chance to have all their friends and families attend this year, with no other school conflicts. It's really the best date for the kids."

People in the crowd began to whisper in excitement about the date change. Of course, they were excited. Monica declared it was the best date "for the kids." Who could argue with that?

Only I knew the truth: Monica was an evil sorceress who had tricked everyone into thinking she was Glinda the Good. They thought this was *The Wizard of Oz* and would break into "Oh What a Celebration" any minute. They didn't realize that this wasn't *The Wizard of Oz*—it was *Wicked*. And I wasn't going to join in their chorus.

"You knew," I said in a loud whisper. My hands shook. "You knew this was the date of my race."

Monica's jaw dropped, but no words came out of her mouth to dispute my accusation. Her silence only confirmed my suspicions.

"I can't believe you would stoop that low," I said, my voice growing louder. "Oh wait... I can. You always do whatever's best, not for the kids, but for *you*."

Several parents gasped. I ignored them. I grabbed my purse, clumsily climbed over the four people in my row, and slammed the doors on my way out of the auditorium.

When I got back to my truck, I buckled my seatbelt forcefully, and sat still for a moment, taking a few deep breaths. My heart raced. My phone vibrated and I rustled through my purse, glad for a distraction.

I glanced at Amelia's text. My eyes filled with tears.

Mom. What in the world was that all about? Thanks a lot.

"Monica strikes again." I wiped my eyes. It looked like my dream day was over before it even started.

~ Six ~

"I was doing a training run late one evening with a guy I was dating, and he accidentally stepped in a hole and fell. When I asked him if he was okay, he said his ankle hurt. I gave him the advice my dad always gave me when I was hurt: 'Just run on it— that will work the soreness out.' The guy called me later that evening from the emergency room where he was being treated for his broken ankle, the very one I had shamed him into running on for about a mile—oops!"
-Annette, runner for over twenty-years

The kids sat in a circle as Fiona read *Chicken Little*. I was still in a daze from the morning and imagined myself as the poor lil' chicken in the story. The sky was falling, thanks to Monica, but no one believed me.

The intercom in our classroom buzzed. "Miss Smith?" Tricia, the front office administrator, spoke through the speaker.

"Yes?" Fiona stopped reading *Chicken Little* and looked up at the speaker.

"We have a new student for your classroom today. Would you send Miss Raymond down to pick her up?"

"I'm on my way." I stood up from my pretzel position on the floor and walked in a daze to the main office. I needed to snap out of it, but I was still so angry at Monica, and at myself for embarrassing

Amelia. Lately, I couldn't do *anything* right.

I opened the door to the main office. *Focus on the task at hand, Kelly Jo*, I admonished myself.

Tricia stood with a small blonde girl. The girl nervously toyed with her backpack straps.

"Meet Taylor Hawkins," Tricia said, and the girl stared at the floor. "She comes all the way from New York."

"Rochester," Taylor whispered to the carpet.

"Welcome to Kentucky," I said to Taylor, trying to sound sweet as pie. It was hard to be the new kid in school, and moving mid-year was especially tough. Helping this girl fit in would be my distraction from thinking about Monica.

The entry door buzzer sounded. I glanced up at the door, and sunbeams surrounded the figure of a man standing in front of Rose Will Elementary School. Here was my new distraction. Erik Wellsworth stood at the front door waiting to come in. I pinched my arm, but it was no dream. He had a white hard hat perched on his head and carried a large white scroll of papers. Tricia buzzed him in.

"Erik, how are you today?" Tricia asked.

She knew him? He knew her?

"I'm great, thanks, Trish. Got some updates for you on construction work. Shutoff schedules, that kind of thing." His sleeves were rolled up, exposing his muscular forearms. He took off his hard hat and ran a hand through his thick hair. I tried not to stare. I failed.

"Wonderful," Tricia chirped. He handed her a stack of papers and she filed them.

He turned to me.

"Good to see you again, Mrs. Kelly Jo…" He paused, waiting for my last name.

"*Miss* Kelly Jo Raymond," I said.

"Youth group," he exclaimed, and snapped his fingers. "I thought I recognized you the other day."

"Yes," I said. "I realized it right after you left. Not that I was watching you from afar."

"Wow." He smiled. "You look great. You haven't changed since high school."

"And you are even more..." I began and broke off. He was more handsome, ripped, gorgeous, and delightfully amazing on the eyes. "You are more of a construction worker than ever," I said after an awkward pause.

"Yes. I work at Wellsworth Construction." He laughed.

"You own your own construction company?"

"Yes, it's just a small company here in Lexington, but I do some business in Dallas, too."

"You're a cowboy?"

I imagined him riding on a horse. A white horse. He would gallop by me, lean down, and swoop me up onto his saddle next to him. We would ride off into the sunset.

He laughed. "Not really a cowboy. But I do like coffee. They like coffee, right? Maybe you'd like to grab a cup with this cowboy impersonator sometime?"

Before I could answer, I heard whimpering.

"Taylor." I turned back to the poor little student, whose eyes were now pooling with tears. I knelt to her level and handed her a tissue.

She clutched her small, brown backpack, and I noticed that it was decorated with horses.

"Do you like horses?" I asked. She frantically nodded. "You're going to love Kentucky," I said while she dabbed her eyes. "My neighbor even has a horse.

Let me tell you about it while we go to your new classroom." I stood and reached for her hand, and she took it, sniffles subsiding.

I glanced back over my shoulder, and Erik had resumed talking with Tricia, but he glanced in my direction.

I smiled back and whispered, "I would love to get coffee. Any time, cowboy."

Taylor kept her little hand in mine, and we walked together down the hallway to the classroom.

When we stepped into the classroom, Fiona and the class turned to look at Taylor.

"This is Taylor Hawkins," I said, and Taylor stared at the floor.

"Welcome to our classroom," Fiona said warmly. "Friends, can you all say hello to Taylor?"

The class all cheered hellos. Taylor rushed to sit on the carpet in the very back and kept her eyes and head down.

"Hi Taylor," JoJo, the smallest and loudest in the class, sang across the room. She was at the kidney table in the corner of the room by herself, which meant she had gotten into trouble again. Bless her heart.

I hung up Taylor's bag and raincoat and walked to the kidney table. I took a seat next to JoJo.

"How's it going?" I whispered.

"I have to sit here because I got in trouble. I wasn't keeping my hands to myself again," she huffed in a loud voice. I put my finger to my lips, motioning for her to be quiet.

"I couldn't help it, Miss Raymond." She continued at full volume in her adorable Kentucky accent. "Sometimes I get steamin' mad at Trey. He makes me really, really, really mad, Miss Raymond.

He's not my friend."

She crossed her little legs. She wore two different colored socks, one hot pink and one striped, looking just like Pippi Longstocking, probably her latest book character fad.

"I understand, JoJo. I really do, honey," I said gently. "Sometimes I get steamin' mad at people, too, especially when they are not being good friends. But you know, we do have to *be* good friends to have good friends."

The argument with Monica still fresh in my mind. I knew too well what JoJo was going through. "Let's pay attention to Miss Smith now," I said to her, and mentally sent a little arrow prayer for JoJo and for myself. We both needed some help today.

"Let's think of some words that rhyme with pail," Fiona said, and several students threw up their hands.

"Sail," Meredith said, and Fiona nodded.

"That's right, sail does rhyme with pail. Can you use it in a sentence?"

Meredith stood up confidently and proudly stated, "I will sail in my boat and put sand in my pail."

"Great work, Meredith. Kiss your brain." Fiona wrote the word "sail" on a small easel.

Meredith smiled, kissed her hand and placed the kiss on her head.

The kids called out more rhyming words.

"Raise your hands so we can hear all your great ideas," Fiona said over the noise.

Leo held one hand in the air and propped it up with his other arm. Fiona pointed to him.

He yelled out, "Fail! I hope I don't fail kindergarten." The kids giggled as Fiona wrote the word on the easel.

"Miss Raymond, Miss Raymond!" JoJo tapped my shoulder frantically. "Kale rhymes with pail."

"You're right." I looked at her incredulously. I never once imagined JoJo eating kale or even knowing about kale.

"Kale," she whispered again, grinning. "Kale rhymes with pail."

"Raise your hand to tell Miss Smith. She'll be so proud. Just think of a sentence." I was so excited for her success and felt so inspired. These were the moments when I realized how much I loved teaching.

JoJo waved her hand in the air, hardly able to contain her excitement.

"I'm gonna kale that stupid ground hog," she whispered in her thick Southern drawl. "That's my sentence."

I grabbed her hand and pulled it down. "Oh, JoJo, no."

"Miss Raymond, I'd never really kale a ground hog. They're really cute. I'm just sayin' it in a sentence," she insisted.

"JoJo, sweetie, that's not the same word. Kale does rhyme with pail, but..."

"I know, Miss Raymond. I'm gonna *kale* that darn ground hog."

"Kale is a green vegetable that you eat, honey. Your word is kill. K-I-L-L."

"I know. Kale!" She beamed and shot her arm back into the air once more.

"JoJo, do you have a word that rhymes with pail?" Fiona asked.

I frantically shook my head back and forth desperately hoping Fiona wouldn't call on her after all.

It didn't matter. At that moment, Andrew yelled, "Hail! Hail rhymes with pail, Miss Smith." All the kids in the classroom *oooed* and *aaahed*.

"That's a bad word," they yelled in chorus.

"No, it's not," I said. "Hail falls from the sky."

The kids turned around and looked at me. "Miss Raymond said a bad word."

JoJo looked up at me with a crazy grin on her face. Even Fiona suppressed an amused smile.

Clearly I needed my own ground hog day. I needed to go back to bed, wake up, and start this day all over again.

Maybe I would start with a new song on my alarm. I was thinking of the Patsy Montana classic, *I Wanna Be a Cowboy's Sweetheart*.

~ Seven ~

"When I'm training, I like to eat almonds—and cheeseburgers!"
-Julia, runner for nine years

The nurse put away her blood pressure monitor.

"My blood pressure is probably off the charts with the past few days I've had," I said. She didn't respond, so I rambled on. "Not to mention, I ran into an old high school friend the other day. He is gorgeous. He would make anyone have high blood pressure."

The nurse looked at me and flicked her eyes back to her computer. "You are here for medical clearance to run a race?"

"Yes, I need to find out if I can run this Jingle Bell 5k race. I won it. On the radio of all places. It's the first prize I have ever won. I've never really run before."

The nurse kept typing. I was sure the nurse was thinking, *bless your heart, there's no way in this world the doctor will clear you to train for this race. You're in the worst shape ever.* She was probably silent because she didn't want to hurt my feelings.

I held my breath while she typed on the computer. High blood pressure would be the perfect excuse to get out of running. No one would tell me I was a quitter if I couldn't run. Then I could go to Amelia's concert, and everything would work out by default. Sure, I wouldn't get to have a dream day, but I would avoid conflict. And exercise.

"My heart is racing pretty fast." I felt my pulse on my wrist. "You know, I could sit out the running portion of this race and let my best friends run it on their own." The nurse remained silent. "Only three people need to show up. But it sounds so amazing."

I sat back in the seat and sighed. Monica made me so mad. She ruined everything. Friendships. Goals. Dreams. I bit my lip and sent up a little arrow prayer. *Dear heavenly Father, please work this situation out.*

The nurse turned to the door, slid her stethoscope into her pocket, and looked back over her shoulder at me. "The doctor will be right in with your results."

"It's bad, isn't it?"

The nurse looked up, her brows knit together, obviously confused by my chipper tone.

"I beg your pardon?"

"My blood pressure. I can't run the race, can I?" I held my breath. The nurse shook her head in what she thought was a reassuring gesture, but it made my stomach sink.

"Your blood pressure is fine, ma'am. Slightly elevated, but that's normal during a doctor's visit. Please wait here on the chair. No need to sit up on the bed. The doctor will be in soon with your results."

I slipped off the examining bed, slumped in the seat, and let out another sigh. Why was I here? I was fooling myself—and everyone else. Even if I was somehow cleared medically, I would never be able to run the race, because I couldn't miss Amelia's senior concert. Monica had completely destroyed my dream day with one little scheduling detail.

I tried to imagine myself running a 5K. Nothing. I squeezed my eyes shut trying to imagine again. This time I thought of Drake's song, *Running to Your Dreams*. I started singing.

"Set your soles on fire.
Blaze ahead at full speed.
Keep your faith alive—as you're running to your dreams."

This time, the image came to me. I could see myself at the starting line. The gun would go off, and I lurched forward with excitement and adrenaline.

Then, I would collide with the person in front of me, lose my balance, and crash to the ground, and break both arms.

After being rushed to the hospital, I would wind up in a body cast from the waist up. Obviously, in my state, my entire Christmas vacation would be spent in traction. Amelia would be by my side, trying to nurse me back to health, and would subsequently miss her college deadlines.

Inspired by the entire debacle, Drake would write a song about his psycho klutz fan who couldn't even run three miles. He would call it, "Crazy Kelly Jo."

The song would be a hit, and Monica would have the a cappella choir sing it for their final concert in the spring. Amelia would get the solo, just to remind her that her mother is a loser.

I took a breath. Clearly, I needed a reality check. I looked around the room, then grabbed my cell phone out of my purse for entertainment while I waited. Daydreams weren't working today.

I scrolled through my newsfeed and felt immediately annoyed. Monica had posted a picture of her and Lindsay on a college visit to NYU. It was marked eight hours ago. I considered calling the nurse back and having her take my blood pressure again, because it sure as heck was rising now. I closed the Facebook™ app and opened Instagram™ instead.

The first picture on my Fid was a picture of Amelia with Lindsay and Amy from the a cappella group. It looked like they were in a music studio.

Amelia never told me she was going to à music studio. In the picture she was wearing headphones and standing by a fancy looking microphone. Amelia's face glowed. *Had they put some filter thingy on this picture?* She was beaming. Amelia's friends, Lindsay and Amy, stood off to the left side, also wearing headphones.

There was someone else in the background, and I expanded the photo to the fullest size to make out the face. My cheeks burned. Monica. *What was she doing at the studio with Amelia? When was this taken, what were they doing, and most important-ly—why didn't I know a dang thing about it?*

"Knock, knock," the doctor said, and pushed open the door. I dropped my phone as if caught in the act of spying.

The doctor, a petite brunette woman in a stiff white coat, picked up the phone, and handed it to me with a little smile. I quickly took it before she could see the evidence of my cyber stalking.

"So, my nurse tells me you need clearance to run a 5K?" The doctor cleared her throat.

"Sort of." All I could think of was the picture of Amelia in that music studio—with Monica and comp-any. I shook my head. I could only focus on one problem at a time, and right now the problem was the race.

"I probably won't be running the race, actually, because my daughter has this thing. But I wanted to get my clearance, just in case. I don't know. It's stupid."

"Actually, it's really good that you came in today," the doctor said, looking at a clipboard. "You haven't been in for a check-up in over six years."

I froze. What was that supposed to mean? Was something wrong? I gripped the sides of the chair, feeling a rush of adrenaline. I took back all my wishes that I would get denied clearance. *Let me be all right, let me be all right,* I prayed silently.

"It turns out that your blood glucose and cholesterol are slightly above normal."

"What in tarnation does that mean?" I said, and the doctor raised both brows and bit her bottom lip, trying to stifle a smile at my reaction. She placed the clipboard in front of me and pointed to a chart.

"It means that you are possibly pre-diabetic, and if you don't get these levels down, we'll have to try some medications for you."

I stared at her speechless again. I wasn't pre-diabetic. I couldn't be. I already had sturdy legs, a half-ass job, and stupid high cholesterol. Now I had *diabetes*, too?

"This is so not fair," I said in frustration.

"The good news is that you may not have to go on medication. It's possible to get your levels down with diet and exercise. These levels are only slightly elevated, Kelly Jo."

"Diet and exercise?" I repeated, dread filling my stomach. Those were not my favorite words, especially coming from a doctor. I preferred words like sugar and shopping.

"Yes. In fact, training for a 5K is a wonderful plan for helping combat this." She paused.

What if I don't run? What if I don't diet? I wanted to ask. Instead I mumbled, "Kale."

"Yes, a healthy diet will help," the doctor said, annoyingly chipper. It was like she was sapping all my happiness and leaving me wilty and gross. Like the salad I was now going to have to eat.

"I'll have the nurse give you a sheet with information about a healthy diet you can follow. With a little bit of exercise, at least three times a week, you'll probably get your numbers back down if you stick to the plan. You should definitely train for this 5K. You're cleared to do so." The doctor signed the dreaded clearance form and offered it to me. I didn't take it. My hands felt glued to my legs. She set it gingerly next to me on the table.

"The nurse will be back to schedule your return visit. I'd like to see you back in four to six weeks for a follow-up. Good luck with the training. It sounds like someone was watching out for you when you won tickets for this 5K. Congratulations."

She glided out of the room, and I sat there stunned like a mule deer in the headlights. Was it a good thing? Was someone watching out for me? I looked up to heaven. *Diet and exercise? Really?*

I closed my eyes and imagined my happy place. Sitting by the fire, drinking a non-diet-approved glass of hot chocolate (with plenty of marshmallows), listening to a CD of Amelia singing, and reading a cozy mystery.

In this daydream Amelia was a famous singer, of course. And I owned a pair of Monica-and-doctor-noise cancelling headphones. Now *that* would be the perfect Christmas.

~ Eight ~

"When I don't feel like running, most of the time I will tell myself, 'you do feel like running.' It's a mind-set thing."
-Sascha, runner for nine years

I sat at the kitchen table and sipped a can of apple-flavored sparkling water.

Amelia stood in front of the pantry, groaned, and then slammed it shut. She wrenched open the refrigerator and stared inside.

The cold air swept into the kitchen, and Amelia groaned again, and slammed the door. She went back to the pantry.

"Ugh."

"Sweetie, Ameils, what are you looking for?" I set down my sparkling water.

"Real cereal, chips, cookies, *something*. There's nothing to eat. Nothing." She waved a hand in front of the pantry, which was practically overflowing. I crossed to the pantry and stood next to her.

"Amelia, there's plenty to eat in here," I said, grabbing box after box and rearranging the food.

"What is this?" She held up a box of fiber cereal and shook it, the flakes rattling inside, an echo of her annoyed mood. She grabbed the box of steel cut oatmeal. "Are we eating rabbit food now? Is this supposed to be my breakfast? Go ahead and call me Peter Cottontail from now on."

"This is pretty good." I lifted my half-empty can of sparkling water and took a swig to prove it. I swallowed too quickly, and choked out, "no calories."

"Mom," Amelia said in exasperation, "it's free of taste, too. Where's my Ale81™? Where's my favorite cola?"

"I need to cut back on sugar," I said gently. "You remember about my visit to the doctor?"

"Momma, *my* cholesterol isn't too high. My glucose isn't too high. This is so not fair," Amelia whined, and I felt a prick of annoyance. Yes, her cholesterol and glucose weren't too high—but someday they would get there, unless I enforced some changes.

"Enough already." I crossed my arms. "It's not like I'm happy about this little situation. Just be glad you don't have to exercise, too."

Amelia flopped into a seat at the table next to me and put her face in her hands. "I feel like someone moved away and I didn't get to say goodbye."

"You and me both, sweetheart," I said, taking another sip of sparkling water. It really wasn't that bad, but I imagined that it was sweet tea. Which was even better.

"I thought you were going to run that race. Won't that cancel out your food or sugar intake or whatever?"

"It doesn't work that way," I sighed, trying not to get caught up in her dramatic attitude. "And besides, I'm not running that race. It's the same night of your concert, *remember*? December sixteenth."

"I don't care if you miss the stupid concert," Amelia said, slumping down even further. "It's not like you think I'm good enough for a career in music, anyway."

"Just because I want you to go to college doesn't mean I don't believe in you, Amelia," I said, trying to resist getting caught up in our usual argument, but feeling the words tumble out of my mouth anyway. "Maybe you could study music at college. Be a music teacher. Do what you love, but get a degree doing it."

"You should go to college. You should finish something. Oh wait, you just want me to finish everything for you," Amelia snapped. "Am I sup-posed to run this race, too?"

She was going for the big punches this morning. And that one hurt.

"Amelia, the race is different. First, I haven't started it. Secondly, I'm not going to miss your last holiday concert," I said in a tone that implied *and that's final*. I crossed to the pantry, pushed past the fiber cereal, and held up another box. "You can eat this. I bought you crispy cereal—you love it, right?"

"Yeah, I loved it when I was two."

"It's really good with strawberries," I offered, presenting the box like Vanna White. She wasn't amused, and I sighed. "Sweetheart, if I keep junk food in the house, I won't be able to resist it. I'll be like Hansel and you'll be like Gretel, and we'll just eat all the junk in the house and not even think about the consequences. I need you try this with me, at least until I go back to the doctor."

"Okay," Amelia said, finally relenting. "I don't want to be eaten by a witch, if you put it that way." She smiled slightly, and I felt a rush of relief. She was on my side, even if she protested. "Wait," Amelia said, interrupting my mental image of us as world-traveling mother-daughter body builders.

"Isn't today the last day to sign up for your race? Isn't that why you went to the sugar-hating doctor to begin with?"

"Were you listening to me at all? I'm not going to skip your concert. I love listening to you sing. I wouldn't miss it."

"If I'm such an amazing singer, why can't I move to Nashville and sing? Monica said..." Amelia broke off, and I squeezed the box of crispy rice, my insides turning to lava. The box crumpled in my grip and the cereal exploded all over the floor with a snap, crackle, and pop.

"Monica said what?" I snapped, not making a move to clean up the mess.

Amelia gasped and pointed at the cereal. "Oh snap. Today is the bake sale," she said, ignoring my question.

"What?" I asked, confused by the sudden change of topic.

"The bake sale. Remember? Did you make anything? You were supposed to bake something to give to the workers while they managed the sale."

We both stared at the mess on the floor.

"You have to bake something that people actually want to eat, mom," Amelia said slowly. "Something with sugar. And I signed you up to work the sale. I saw Monica's name right next to yours. I didn't do that on purpose, so don't freak out again. She signed up after I signed you up."

"I'll bake something that everyone will want to eat, even Monica. And I'm not missing your concert. And I'm not running that race. And you're going to college," I said, shaking. Shaking from lack of sugar, and because even though my words sounded firm, I was a bubble of uncertainty. What was Monica telling

69

Amelia that Amelia didn't want me to know?

"Why should I go to college? You didn't finish. You just dream about it," Amelia added punch number seventeen.

A car horn honked from outside, and Amelia's phone buzzed.

"I gotta go. Amy's here," she said, grabbing her backpack, and heading out the door.

I ran after her and shoved an apple in her hand. "You didn't have breakfast. At least take some fruit."

Amelia glanced at the apple. "Yummy," she said in a dull, unenthusiastic voice, and then walked down the sidewalk.

I sighed, and then turned back to the pantry. I stepped over the cereal and gazed inside. *What can I bake?* Nothing in the pantry looked appetizing. I stepped closer trying to find something that would give me inspiration. My foot slipped and the cereal on the floor crunched. I glanced down at the cereal all over the floor, getting an idea.

~ Nine ~

"I think a lot of people don't give themselves enough time to really enjoy running, because often times it's harder before it gets easier. Also, some days you just have a bad day, and you feel crappy through your whole run, or you have a terrible race. It doesn't mean you're not a runner, or that you're not improving. You just have to keep going."
-Cheryl, runner for twenty-six years

The end of the school day was always a restless shuffle of stuffing folders in backpacks, handing out daily stars, and trying to keep students engaged for the last twenty minutes.

This Friday was no different: I tried to organize the backpacks, while Fiona gathered the students around on the floor, so they could listen to her read *If You Give a Moose a Muffin.*

The kiddos wriggled around, restless. The sugar rush from lunch boxes full of Halloween candy was tangible in the classroom. Trey bounced his Fit on the band attached to his desk and twirled his fidget spinner. JoJo braided and re-braided her Pippi Longstocking hairdo. Only Taylor was quiet.

I felt a rush of guilt. Taylor still wasn't fitting in, and I hadn't been able to find her a friend yet. But I just didn't have the kids' energy. My morning had been stressful, what with Amelia's attitude and our exhausting continual argument, and I was so ready for the weekend. I focused on finishing up the folders. I needed to get going. I had to stop by the bake sale first and sell whatever with Monica. Then I was going to head home and collapse.

An agitated noise broke me out of my thoughts. Andrew raised his hand, trying to get Fiona's attention. "Miss Smith. Miss Smith!"

"Andrew, please keep your hands in your basket while we read," Fiona said patiently. "We'll ask questions after the story is over." Andrew's face went white.

"Miss Smith, my tummy feels sick. *Really* sick."

I threw the folders in a heap on top of the cubbies, knowing that when a kindergartener said they feel *really sick*, you better listen—I had learned that one fast. I leaped over a desk, hoping my super-power of speed would intervene in time.

"Come with me, sweetie," I said, putting my hands on Andrew's shoulders and moving him along quickly toward the door while maintaining at least a facade of calmness.

I guided him out of the classroom, and Fiona mouthed a silent *thank you*.

I walked Andrew down the hall, and calmly whispered, "Do you feel like you're going to throw up, sweetie?"

He looked up at me and nodded. Then he leaned forward and threw up all over my favorite gold ballet flats.

The end-of-the-day announcements came over the intercom, our principal's chipper voice filled the hall.

"It has been a great week at Rose Will Monroe Elementary."

Andrew sniffled, drowning out the rest of the announcements.

"It's okay, honey. We'll get this all cleaned up,

and everything will be okay," I said, mentally adding *buy new shoes* to my never-ending to-do list.

~ * ~

I rushed to my car, still smelling a faint scent of vomit. Andrew was on his way home, thankfully feeling much better, but now I was fabulously and terribly late for the bake sale.

I covered my mouth with one hand, stifled another gag from the smell of the vomit, and glanced at my watch. I had seven minutes to get to the a cappella bake sale—a practically impossible feat.

There was one silver lining from the whole vomit incident—there was no temptation for me to want to eat or buy any of the desserts at the upcoming bake sale. I had no appetite.

I made it to the bake sale, much more than fashionably late. Monica glanced at her phone. Great. We were volunteers together.

Are you trying to teach me something? I don't think I ever prayed for patience, I asked silently, gazing at heaven.

"I didn't think you were going to show up," Monica said tartly. "Amelia told me you worked today, so I guess that's why—" she stopped mid-sentence and glanced at my blouse, raising her perfectly threaded brows. "Oh, were you running? Were you working out?"

"Oh, no. That? That's nothing." I lied, folding my arms in front of my silk shirt. There was a wet stain down the front, where I had washed out Andrew's vomit with a Tide-to-go™.

"I'm surprised you're still training," Monica said. "Since the race is the same day of the concert. I didn't know before, but it's a shame." Her voice

73

dripped with fake sincerity.

I took a seat at the table and said nothing, because I couldn't think of a nice response. Monica would do anything to sabotage me.

Monica went on, despite my silence. "What are you going to do? Are you actually going to miss Amelia's final Holiday Concert to run the race?"

I waited. No booming answer from God. I knew this situation needed a miracle, so it was going to have to come from him, but it hadn't arrived yet.

"Bless your heart, Kelly Jo, you have too much on your plate with work, college visits, and Amelia's concert," Monica said. It was amazing how much she could talk, with no encouragement from me. "I have no idea how you have any time to even think about training for a 5K. It's probably best that you forget that crazy dream." She paused. "I hope you didn't think that I had anything to do with the date—it was the drama club. They beat me to the calendar and booked up the entire month of November. Something about that construction work next door and access to the parking lot. I tried to explain at the meeting, but you..."

She stopped mid-sentence and her eyes met mine for a moment.

I felt a flash of guilt. Maybe Monica *didn't* book the December date on purpose.

"I really didn't have anything to do with it, Kells," she said, somehow reading my mind.

She never called me Kells. At least not in the last seventeen years. She sounded like her old self.

I let out a small sigh. I hadn't realized I was holding my breath.

"You know Kells, Amelia is a good singer," Monica said in a soft voice. "Really good."

"Thank you, Monica. That's really nice of you to say." I managed.

"Raymond women are good at fighting for what really matters. She's always standing up for what she wants. She got that from you, didn't she?"

I couldn't tell if she was being sarcastic. Was I teaching Amelia that Raymond women are good at fighting for what matters? Through my own life?

Even if Amelia's concert hadn't been scheduled for the same day as the race, I probably would've found another excuse to get out of running.

I thought again about winning the tickets for the dream day with Drake Douglas, and the Jingle Bell Run, and suddenly it hit me. I really wanted my prize. I actually wanted to run. I needed to run.

"Monica, would you mind working the bake sale by yourself?" I bumped the table in my haste to stand. "I have something to do."

Monica put a hand on a plate of lemon squares to stop them from falling off the edge.

"Sure, Kelly Jo." She blinked in surprise. "But we're not going to make any money for the Holiday Spectacular if people aren't here to run the bake sale. We need those new dresses—you know, some girls need bigger sizes, and we just don't have the money unless we sell—"

"I'm sure you can manage," I interrupted. "And you're right. Raymond women are fighters. Thank you for that too, Monica."

I put a pan of crispy treats on the table. "These are for you. I remember how you used to love these when we were in college."

I turned away and ran, praying as I rushed to my truck.

I'm sorry. I know that I shouldn't have given

those crispy treats to Monica. But I just couldn't resist. Lord, I do need forgiveness. And I've been a horrible mother, too. I need to teach Amelia to fight—and run with perseverance.

I started up my truck, plugged in my cell phone to the audio cord in the lighter charger, and searched my music. I selected *Wide Open Spaces* and turned the volume to full blast. The tires on my truck squealed as I drove out of the high school parking lot. I needed to get to the radio station. It was time to get out of this dang rut.

~ Ten ~

"I went the wrong way during a 5K one time. I was with a girl on the cross-country team, and we were running one way, and then we realized there was a turn, and we had gone around the wrong way!"
-Cassidy, runner for three years

I drove carefully, trying not to speed. My heart raced fast enough to power a car in the Indy 500. I had to pick up the tickets by 5:00 p.m., and I wouldn't make it unless I hit every green light.

I shot up another arrow prayer: *Dear Lord, if this is meant to be, please help me get there on time.*

I envisioned myself racing into the office and picking up the tickets.

"You're Kelly Jo?" they would ask. I would waltz in, wearing a dazzling blouse with a jeweled neckline and cowboy boots. "Drake will be so happy to hear that you've won."

I would toss my hair and flash them a winning smile. "Lil' old me?" I'd say with a shrug. "Oh, I win all the time. I guess I just have amazing luck."

Then I'd climb into the back of a tractor filled with hay, tickets in hand, and it would take off into the sunset with Drake Douglas's song blasting through the speakers.

I blinked. I stared at the back of a tractor filled with hay, but it wasn't in my mind's eye anymore—it was real. I was stuck behind an actual tractor, which was trudging along at twenty miles under the speed

77

limit.

"No!" I smacked my hands on the wheel. "No, no, no." I stared at the clock. I was running out of time. There was no way I would make it unless I got past the tractor.

I sped up, thinking that maybe I could pass it, but then I spotted a cop car clocking just ahead and quickly took my foot off the gas. If I got pulled over, I definitely wouldn't make it.

I tapped my hands on the steering wheel. I swerved out a little to the other side of the road and then quickly back to my side. A red sporty sedan whisked past me. I peeked around the tractor again. I held my breath, hit the gas pedal, and sped quickly past, slipping back into my own lane. I was going to get those tickets.

I pulled into the radio station office and parked haphazardly across two spaces. Not bothering to fix the crooked car, I slammed the door shut and rushed inside.

I ran into the building at a full-on sprint, breathing heavily, and burst through the front doors.

A receptionist sat at a large front desk, talking on a phone. There was a large clock on the wall above her.

It read: 5:05 p.m. I was too late.

I wilted, and my purse slipped off my shoulder and smacked the floor. Despite everything, despite my resolve to actually *do* something for once, I had failed because of a dang *tractor*. This couldn't be happening. *Lord, I guess this is my answer.*

"No, you listen, Trent," the receptionist yelled into the phone. "I'm not going to say this again. We are over. Stop calling me at work. If you really want to get back together, I suggest you quit spending so much time playing stupid video games and remember my birthday for once."

A woman with a cropped bob rounded the corner and leaned against the reception desk. "Christine, is this a personal call?"

The receptionist quickly hung up the phone. "It's my ex. I told him to stop calling me." She looked up and spotted me. "Oh *no*. How long have you been standing there? I'm so sorry—this is so embarrassing. My ex-boyfriend forgot my birthday, and it's just this whole big thing." She shuffled some papers on the front desk, cheeks pink.

It was a miracle. I glanced toward heaven and smiled. This was my moment. *Thank you.*

"Christine?" I asked.

"Yes?"

"I am so sorry about your ex, but you're right. You have every right to be upset. Birthdays are important. And no need to apologize to me. I'm here to pick up tickets, and I'm not worried at all about waiting."

"Are you Kelly Jo Raymond? The one who won the Drake Douglas tickets?" The woman with the bob turned in my direction and extended her hand. "I'm Barb, Barb Huntington, and I manage all the contests. We're usually very strict with those deadlines, but since Christine kept you waiting," she said giving Christine a stern look, "of course we'll get them for you. Just follow me."

Hardly believing this random stroke of good luck, I glanced at Christine and smiled before I followed Barb to the back, where she handed me a large envelope labeled "Kelly Jo Raymond—contest winner."

"Inside you'll find your tickets and the race

packet. All the information you need to know about the race, concert, and the overall dream day with Drake is in there. I apologize again for our receptionist. She's usually very organized and dependable. But you know how kids and their boyfriends can be." Her eyes darted in concern, and she furrowed her brow when she looked up at me, waiting for my response. I beamed back at her.

"I know exactly how they can be. No worries at all."

Her whole body relaxed, and her eyes brightened. "Enjoy your day, Ms. Raymond."

"Thank you, I absolutely will."

I practically floated out of the office, my legs still burning from my mad dash to get inside, making a mental note the whole way back to my car to send Christine a birthday present myself.

~ Eleven ~

"You always feel good after you run. It helps with everything—energy, your own self-image, body image, being productive, and taking time for yourself."
-Laura, runner for ten years

I arrived at school on Monday, walking taller and with a bounce in my step. I hadn't felt this much energy and excitement in months—maybe years. I was doing something *for me*. And it felt great.

I rushed down the hallway to our kindergarten classroom. I couldn't wait to tell Fiona I had picked up the tickets on Friday and the race was a go. I hadn't told her yet, because I wanted to see her face-to-face when she heard the news. Sure, I still had no idea what I was going to do about Amelia's conflicting concert time, but like my momma always said, "Don't you worry your little head about tomorrow. Make a choice about the now and don't look back."

The students were arriving and hanging up their coats when I entered the room. I was distracted, and I could barely focus on helping them. JoJo waved her folder in front of my face.

"My mom read me so many books this weekend," she said, and launched into a long-winded description of a fantasy book about a princess befriending a unicorn.

Taylor stood behind JoJo, listening intently to the story. I was glad *someone* listened, because I

81

couldn't focus. All I could think of was training, Drake Douglas, the concert, and the race.

I imagined holding out my hand to meet him. He would gently grasp my hand and pull it to his lips for a gentle kiss.

I stood near the coat cubbies lost in my dream.

"Kells?" Fiona asked. "What's up?" She was at the front of the room, writing on the chalkboard. I snapped out of my daydream and rushed over to her. I felt like a kid, itching to tell her the good news.

"Fiona, I did it," I said in a low voice, and she turned to me, confused.

"Did what?"

"I went to the radio station and got the tickets. Get out your favorite Christmas running clothes because the race is on, girlfriend."

Taylor suddenly walked up to Fiona and tugged on her skirt.

"Just a minute, Taylor," Fiona said. She turned back to me and raised her hand to for a high five. "I can't believe this. We're going to meet Drake Douglas."

"Miss Smith, I don't feel so good," Taylor said insistently, tugging on Fiona's skirt over and over again.

Fiona held up one finger. "Just one second, sweetie."

"I hate to miss Amelia's performance," I said, an idea coming to me, "but what if I go to the dress rehearsal? That's it. That's what I'll do. Things are turnin' around, Fi."

"Miss Smith!"

It wasn't Taylor's quiet voice this time—several of the kids yelled out and backed away. The scene unfolded in slow motion—Taylor covered her mouth,

82

raced to the trash can and threw up everywhere.

The kids rushed to get a look.

"Oh, my heavens, no. Get back, friends." I hurried over. "Go to your seats. Now."

I silently berated myself for ignoring the cardinal rule of kindergarten when it came to vomit. The second rule also sprung to mind—if one kid throws up, someone else will eventually follow. We had a stomach bug on our hands.

"I'll take care of it," I told Fiona, and rushed Taylor out of the classroom before anything else could go wrong.

We made our way to the nurse's office, where two other students sat, pale and crying. Looked like I was right: there was something going around.

Taylor gasped in between sniffles, and I felt a pang of sympathy for the little kid. Being sick was never fun.

Nurse Tanya came out of her office holding a sniffling little girl's hand.

"Miss Raymond, would you mind sitting here with Taylor and these kiddos while I go take Bonnie Sue to the main office? Her mom is here," Tanya said to me, clearly stressed. I nodded quickly.

"Thank you," she said, and rushed out the door with Bonnie Sue, leaving me with Taylor and another little boy. They both looked pale and scared, and I spoke in a reassuring tone.

"It's okay, guys. We'll call home for you. You'll feel better soon."

"You can't call my mom to come get me," Taylor said miserably. "Please don't."

"We have to, hon," I said, growing concerned. Why didn't she want us to call her momma?

"She had to go to the gym today, Miss Raymond.

She said she really needed to, or she would 'splode. My grandma and grandpa are coming for Thanksgiving, and she said she was going to 'splode because she had so much to do." She looked up, eyes wide. "I don't want my mom to 'splode."

Ah. I grinned, suddenly realizing Taylor's mis-understanding.

"She won't explode, sweetie," I told her, trying not to laugh. "She's gonna be fine. That's just an expression. Everything will be all right with your momma—and with you, too." I handed her another tissue and patted her on the back.

"I don't know," she said, taking the tissue. "Nobody is my friend."

"You'll find friends," I said quickly, feeling another pang of guilt that I hadn't achieved my mission to help Taylor fit in. "It just takes time."

"Everybody else just wants to color or play tag during recess. Nobody plays horses with me," she said sadly. "Maybe I should just color."

"We'll find someone who wants to play horses," I said confidently. "Sometimes you just have to start doing it yourself, and people will join in."

Tanya rushed back into the room. "Thank you, Kelly Jo," she said, nodding to the kids. "It's crazy here today. I can take care of these friends now."

She squatted, feeling Taylor's forehead. I couldn't help noticing Tanya's muscular calves as she balanced on her black Mary Jane designer working shoes.

"Tanya, you're a runner, aren't you?" I asked. She stuck a thermometer in Taylor's ear.

"I try to run at least three or four times a week," she said, and examined the thermometer.

"What kind of sneakers do you use?"

She looked up. "Nike Pegasus™. Are you a runner?" She looked at my face as she spoke, not at my "sturdy" legs, and I felt a rush of gratitude.

"I am. Or at least, I'm about to be. I just decided to run a 5K." Pride bloomed in my chest. *I could do this.* "I'm running it this December. It's kind of a crazy story, but yeah. I guess I'm a runner now."

"You really are a go-getter, Kelly Jo, that's what I like about you. If you ever need a running partner, give me a call." She leaned over and whispered, "Studies show it increases your libido, too—not a bad side effect!"

I laughed. "I've never done anything like this before."

"Do you feel like you're going to 'splode?" Taylor piped in.

"Yes, in a way, hon, but in a good way." I told her, unable to stifle a laugh this time.

~ Twelve ~

*"My mom tried to stop me from running. She
said it's bad for your 'female organs.'"*
-Joni, runner for five years

Once Taylor was on her way home to her
sympathetic mom—who definitely wasn't mad, only
concerned—I took off down the hallway, a surge of
excitement growing once more. I would check out
the shoes Tanya recommended: Nike Pegasus™. I
liked the name. It reminded me of Greek goddesses.

I imagined myself inclined on a sofa with my legs
crossed, bouncing a sneakered foot gently up and
down. A tall, dark, and handsome man in a toga
would stand over me, gently feeding me
strawberries. Chocolate-covered strawberries.
*Delicious. And the strawberries wouldn't be bad,
either.*

I stepped into the classroom. The students were
at their desks, math cubes scattered everywhere for
their latest lesson.

"Olivia, could you collect the cubes?" Fiona
asked. Olivia rushed to pick up the bucket. Always
the helper, Leo jumped out of his chair and collided
with Olivia in the process. The tub full of colorful
math cubes flew all over the floor.

The whole thing reminded me of bumping into
Erik Wellsworth. I had missed an opportunity. When I
bumped into him, I should have cleaned off that
starched white shirt of his. It was the perfect excuse
to touch his strong muscular arms, or better yet, his

chest.

I shook my head. What in the world was I doing? First, I was daydreaming about running like a goddess, and now I was fantasizing about Erik during math centers. I really needed to pull myself back to reality. I had too much to do, between work and my new training plan, to sit around thinking up crazy stories in my mind. *But one more daydream for the road,* I told myself. I closed my eyes. I imagined Erik as the toga-clad man feeding me, the running goddess, chocolate-covered strawberries.

"We've got this, guys. No worries. Let's clean it up together and count them as we go," I said quickly, trying to refocus.

Olivia picked up cubes right away, singing while she worked, and surprisingly, Leo helped her.

"Everyone else, line up for a bathroom break," Fiona said, shepherding kids into a line.

"I can take care of that, too," I said quickly. "I'll take them." I locked the lid shut and slid the math bucket onto the shelf. I walked to the front of the line.

"Thank you, Miss Raymond. I'll get their writing centers ready while you go," Fiona said. She was always so organized and prepared.

I led the kids down the hall to the bathroom. They laughed and bumped into each other more than usual while we walked. "Okay, let's catch our bubbles in our mouths, friends."

Several kids stopped talking and pretended to catch a big bubble and puffed out their cheeks. Two boys hopped on one foot down the hallway. One girl continued walking but decided to walk backwards. It seemed they were more energetic than usual—but then I noticed JoJo near the back of the line. She walked silently with her hands folded in front of her, looking down at the floor. I wondered what was bothering her today.

"Let's play the statue game," I said when we arrived at the opening near the bathrooms. "One, two, three, everybody freeze." My whole class froze in place. The two boys tried to freeze standing on one foot. "Okay, you can go in now. Remember, only five at a time. Don't forget to wash your hands."

The kids filed into the restrooms, and I stood against the wall. The kids waiting to go in were staying frozen. It worked. I pulled my phone out and scrolled through Lululemon™.

I needed to shop for training clothes. The race preparations called for a whole new wardrobe. It wasn't daydreaming if I was shopping. I was completing an errand.

I could see myself running past the coffee shop with Lululemon™ running pants and a jog bra. I'd run in slow motion, and everyone would stop to stare. They would take note of my fit core and shapely legs. With my dream still in mind, I glanced up at my reflection in the glass of the maintenance closet door. I was surely getting ahead of myself. Me in a jog bra. Now *that* would get some attention.

JoJo tapped me on the arm.

"Line up when you're done, sweetie," I told her absentmindedly. I scanned the store's sale section on my phone. *So many options. Zebra or leopard-print running pants?* I hovered over the add to cart image. *Would the stripes emphasize my legs too much? Polka-dots?*

"Miss Raymond. We're done," Olivia said loudly, pulling me out of my runner's shopping spree.

"Great. Let's tiptoe back like lil' mice." I

shoved my phone into my pocket and led the kids tiptoeing down the hallway, back into the room.

"I didn't hear y'all come in, you were so quiet," Fiona declared. The kids giggled and headed toward their seats. I was glad to see their frantic energy subside.

"Okay, friends, it's time for centers," Fiona told the kids, clapping her hands. "Olivia and Leo, you go to computers first. Timothy, Taylor, Natalie, and Will, you get to go to the writing tables."

"Miss Raymond. Miss Raymond," Leo called out. "Will you help me log onto the computer?"

I walked over and knelt next to him, suddenly noticing an empty little chair. It was JoJo's seat—but she was nowhere in sight.

"Leo, have you seen JoJo?"

"No, Miss Raymond," Leo mumbled, distracted by the computer screen. "Can you help me now?"

"Hold on one second, sweetie," I said, and rushed over to Fiona, whispering in a low voice, "JoJo's missing."

"Oh, this is horrible. This is really bad. Principal Lou is going to be furious. This is the second time we've lost a student, Kelly Jo. What are we going to do?" Fiona said urgently.

Guilt blossomed in my stomach. "It's my fault. I should've been paying more attention during the bathroom break. She must have wandered off," I said, reaching up and pulling my ponytail holder tighter. "I'll find her. I'll go look right now. I've got this, Fi. It's going to be fine. Just fine."

"I'll call Lou so he can make an announcement," Fiona said, her voice slightly icy.

I could tell she was annoyed with me, and I felt another rush of guilt. Why couldn't I do anything right lately?

"I'll take care of it," I insisted. "It was my mistake. I'll call Lou."

I grabbed my cell phone and called the main office as I headed out of the room. I sent up a quick arrow prayer for help. *Dear Lord, please help me find this little girl.*

The intercom screeched while I jogged down the hallway, searching every corner for any sign of JoJo.

"JoJo Henry, please report immediately to the front office. Teachers, this is a code three—if you see JoJo, please escort her immediately to the front office."

Where would I go if I were a kindergartener? I clenched my eyes shut and imagined running out of the building to freedom. Seeing an ice cream truck. Crossing into the street where—oh dear. I snapped my eyes open. *Stay calm. Don't panic. Not yet.*

Every single student loved gym, right? I headed there and looked all over, but there was no sight of JoJo.

Maybe she went back outside to the playground. Yes, the playground.

I took off down the hallway, but when I passed the water fountain, a student yelled, "We aren't supposed to run in the hallways."

"You're so right," I said, but internally added, *you little stinker.*

I speed-walked down the hallway in the direction of the playground. Suddenly, I heard a little cough and sob. I froze. I heard it again. It seemed like it was coming from the library, and I glanced in the windows.

The librarian silently shelved books in the corner, but I couldn't see anyone else inside. I must have imagined it, and chanted to myself, *stay focused*.

I spun around and nearly collided with Principal Lou.

His drill-sergeant type face contorted into an expression of rage at the sight of me.

"Miss Raymond—" His mustache bristled.

"Lou, I'm so sorry. I will find her. I'm looking for her right now," I said frantically.

"Miss Raymond, we can't have our children lost in this school. We need to know where they are at all times. This is unacceptable."

"I'm on it, sir. She's an imaginative little girl, and she probably just..." I trailed off, unable to think of what else to say.

"Let me know the second you find her." He briskly turned and marched down the hallway sending a rush of cold air in my direction.

I heard the cough again, and this time, I was sure it wasn't just my imagination. *It had to be her. She loved the library.*

"JoJo," I called, once inside the library. She didn't answer. The librarian looked up and held a finger to her lips, her eyes like daggers.

"A student is missing," I snapped.

How would I ever be able to handle the full responsibility of a classroom? Even a trip to the bathroom was too difficult for me. Maybe I wasn't teacher material after all.

Sniff. The noise came from the checkout desk area, and I darted over. There, under the table, JoJo was huddled with her arms around her legs and tears streaming down her face.

"JoJo, sweetie, what are you doing? I've been looking everywhere for you." With a sense of immediate relief, I crawled under the table and sat next to her.

"Everybody keeps leaving, so I wanted to leave, too," JoJo said in between sniffs.

"Taylor left because she was sick, sweetie." I moved a little closer and wrapped my arm around her shoulders.

"I wanted to run away like the unicorns in the story," JoJo said firmly, wiping her tears. "I was going to tell you about it, but you were on your phone."

"Oh, JoJo, I'm sorry. I should've been paying attention to you. But now lots of people are looking for you, and I need to let them know. I'll use my phone just to let everyone know you are okay, and then put it away." I pulled it out and showed her, and then texted Fiona, *I found her.* "I need to let Principal Lou know you're okay, too," I told JoJo. I texted Lou. "You can't run away like that, sweetie."

"Isn't that what you were gonna do with those new clothes and sneakers?"

She must have seen my phone screen when I was online shopping. I pursed my lips. If I wasn't so relieved, guilt-stricken, and stressed out, I might have laughed.

"Oh, JoJo, I'm not going anywhere." I saw Principal Lou coming toward the library. "At least, I hope not."

~ Thirteen ~

"I won a pair of running shoes at a race once. They advertised that the winner of every age group would win a free pair of running shoes, and I needed a pair of running shoes. It was a good year, because as you get older, if you're the youngest in the age group you do better, and I did—I won!"
-Tanya, runner for twenty-two years

"What horrible luck that the Holiday Spectacular and your 5k are on the same exact night, and almost the same time to boot. Who'd ever guess that such a horrible thing could happen? You probably couldn't run it anyway, with those legs," I continued. "You can't finish anything. Besides, I'm the runner, and I'm the one who wins at everything."

I sarcastically mimicked Monica's high-pitched voice while I rifled through my closet. She didn't sound as shrill as my impression, but a girl could dream.

I pushed aside a pile of cardigans and unearthed a brown package. It had been delivered earlier in the week, but I hadn't had time to open it. Excitement built in my chest at the prospect of examining the contents.

Fiona told me where to buy great running clothes. After school, I immediately ordered some online. I wasn't going to make that mistake again.

I pulled open the box, happy that at least one part of the whole running thing was guaranteed to be fun. Shopping.

I opened the package and held up a pair of new running pants. *These will surely make me look like a runner.* I held them up and they looked incredibly small. *Maybe they're supposed to be super tight. At least they'll keep everything snug, if I can squeeze into them.*

I envisioned myself running in the tiny black pants. In my vision, my legs looked amazing, like Carrie Underwood's. I imagined Erik Wellsworth jogging past me, doing a double take, and turning around to jog along with me. We'd jog for hours, talking, laughing, and running right into the sunset. It would be perfect.

I stripped off my work clothes and pulled on the pants, breathing heavily. *Oh heavens, this is a workout just getting these pants on,* I thought. I jumped up and down slightly, tugging them on one inch at a time. I stiffly walked over to my full-length mirror.

My stomach bulged out the top of the pants. I yanked the pants up higher. The bulge moved up. No Carrie Underwood's sexy legs, tight butt, or even ankles. No possibility of running into the sunset with a gorgeous guy with these pants.

"Maybe it works with the whole outfit," I mumbled, refusing to be discouraged. I grabbed the hot pink sports bra I'd ordered and slipped it over my head, but it got stuck at my face. It was so tight that it wouldn't move. I pulled one arm through at a time. My boobs looked like one big blob.

I reached for the last bag in the box and pulled out my new zebra print running top. Maybe the zebra stripes would distract anyone from seeing my muffin top.

"Muffin top," I mumbled to myself, putting on

the shirt. "I'd kill for a chocolate-chip one right about now."

I turned to the mirror again. I wasn't the fairest of them all—despite the tightness of the pants, my legs still looked sturdy, and the top didn't conceal unflattering bulges. Even so, I felt a little sweet pang of pleasure, because I realized that I kind of looked like a runner. I posed in a running position in front of the mirror and ran in slow motion in front of the mirror. *I don't just look like a runner. I am a runner.*

I realized I wasn't breathing. I tried to take a deep breath. I couldn't.

"They're cutting off my circulation." I gasped and shifted the waistline back down. I felt like a Victorian lady swooning from a corset laced too tight.

"*Ugh*," I moaned, realizing that my moment of glory was over. I rummaged around my dresser for a pair of white socks.

"Darn it all." I had no socks, at least, no athletic socks. I never bought socks for sneakers, because I never wore sneakers. I settled for a pair of polka-dot navy dress socks. I glanced at myself in the mirror and didn't know whether to laugh or cry. I looked completely ridiculous—zebra-print top, pink jog bra, polka-dot, black muffin-top-producing running pants, and navy-blue polka-dot socks.

But Cinderella had a trick up her sleeve. I still had my best-for-last box. I pulled out the goddess box, opened it, and immediately felt my mood lift as I slipped on my brand-new black, pink-striped sneakers.

"Take that Monica. POW!" I kicked my leg out to

the side in a power kick and then doubled over, holding my thigh. *"Ow."*

Leave it to me to pull a muscle before I even started my first training run.

I walked gingerly down the hall and knocked on Amelia's door. "Honey, I'm heading out for my run."

"I'm almost ready."

"Ready?" I said, confused. Was Amelia coming on the run with me? Maybe she was more supportive than I thought.

Amelia threw open her door, dressed in a flannel top and jeans. "Mom, what are you wearing? Why do you keep doing this?" She looked me up and down, taking in my odd ensemble. "I mean, I get that the dermatologist isn't a five-star resort, but are you sure you don't want to change into something a little more normal?"

"The dermatologist?" I repeated, my heart sinking. I had completely forgotten Amelia had an appointment this morning. I had to get a planner. Today.

"I need to get the wart on my foot frozen off before college," Amelia said urgently. "You didn't forget, did you? You not only want me to go to college, but you want me to go with a wart on my foot? Everyone will talk about me. No one will room with me."

Where was that stinkin' fairy godmother of mine? I was wearing my glass slippers, but I still didn't get to go to the ball. At least the sneakers had made me feel powerful, if only for a minute. *Wait. Why can't I go to the ball?*

"Sweetheart, is there any way someone else could take you? I'm supposed to start my training today." I never suggested she get a ride if I was available. This was new territory, but I was excited to try and start something for myself. I was grasping at straws. Amelia started to get upset.

"Momma, you know I hate needles. They're going to give me a shot in my foot—not to mention, this whole thing is so *embarrassing*. You're not really going to go on a fun run with your girlfriends, while I get a needle shoved in my foot, are you?"

I couldn't think of anything to say. But I bit my lip and nodded my head yes.

"You said you were just running with the girls for fun," Amelia went on. "You aren't running the 5K anyway. You can miss one run."

"I guess I didn't tell you—"

"What would it hurt to miss one training run? Besides, you're not really a runner, Momma. You don't exercise. Ever."

"It's just, it's my first day of training," I said desperately. "Couldn't you drive yourself? Wear slippers? I must go on this run today, Amelia. It's my first day. And it turns out that I *am* going to run the 5k."

"What? How can you run it? It's the same night of the Holiday Spectacular. *My* senior Holiday Spectacular."

"Amelia, I know, and I'm sorry but I realized I can go to your dress rehearsal. I'll be there for that, and then I'll make sure that I'm at your spring recital. It works out perfectly."

"Momma, you're so, so selfish. Is that how you want me to be?"

I stood for a moment imagining a future where thirty-five-year-old Amelia stomped her foot in this way, with her boss watching in shock.

"Today, I'm going to go for my first training run,"

I said firmly, "and you're going to go to the derma-tologist on your own."

"Are you kidding me? Are you serious? I can't drive myself."

"Amelia, I love you, and you can do this. And you know what? It will make you a stronger person. Raymond women know what they want, and they go for it."

Amelia started to complain again, but I cut her off. "You want this wart off? Pull up your big girl panties and go get it removed. I'll see you later and you can tell me all about it. I've got a training run to get to. Love you."

I kissed Amelia on the head, grabbed my water bottle, and headed out the door.

~ Fourteen ~

"I'm not the person to ask about advice on drinking water, because the first thing I pop open after a run is a Diet Coke."
-Joni, runner for five years

I pulled into the athletic center parking lot and swigged one last drink from my new Hydro-Flask™ water bottle.

I'm totally killing this whole training thing. I've got this. I can totally do this. Just one more to go for the entire day.

Tossing the water-bottle on the passenger seat, I thought, *this new routine is gonna be a piece a cake.* I wouldn't think about all the exercise, instead, I would focus on the positive. I can easily drink my allotted amount of water, my friends would be running by my side, and we could all talk and possibly have fun while we ran.

Fiona, Shruti, and Georgia stood together in a group on the sidewalk, looking like a line of little ducks. Fiona waved her arms in crazy circles around her head, stretching. Georgia talked animatedly, and Shruti nodded her head in response.

Stepping out of the vehicle in my new running sneakers, I felt a surge of energy, but the second I stepped out, I slipped on a pile of loose gravel and crumpled to the ground beside my truck.

"I'm all right," I said, still lying on the ground, sure that my friends had witnessed the whole thing.

I rolled over on my side and saw a swish at eye

level. The stripe wasn't black with a cute pink stripe like mine, but green. Green as the Wicked Witch of the West. I followed the shoe up a shapely leg, which was attached to Monica. Framed by sunlight, she stood tipping above like a house about to fall directly on me.

"Bless your heart, it's you, Kelly Jo," she said in a voice I knew I would mimic later. "For a second I thought you were Amy's nana. She walks here regularly, and she wears *fun* tops like that too."

I stared at her, speechless. Amy's nana was eighty-two years old. Did I seriously look like her?

Monica placed her hands on her knees and leaned down to get a closer look. "So, you're really running now?"

Her icy blue eyes took in my zebra-top and polka-dot black pants, landing on my polka-dot navy-blue socks. Why did I wear this outfit? Of course, *she* looked gorgeous in her outfit, since the tight fabric flattered her figure instead of turning it into baked goods.

I bit my tongue and glanced up to Heaven. *Please help me to keep my big mouth shut. And help me to be kind, because right now I can't think of even one nice little thing to say.* Why did I seem to be sending up so many of those arrow prayers lately?

I stood up and brushed gravel off my butt. Monica remained towering over me. She continued to survey the scene, seemingly unable to translate my silence into my real thoughts. *Go. Away.*

"Are you still training for that Elf Jingle Dash?" Monica asked in mock surprise. "Don't tell me you're going to miss Amelia singing for her senior year holiday concert? You surprise me, Kells. You never miss anything Amelia does—at least, I didn't think you did."

I shrugged. *Be kind. Don't say anything.*

"Or wait, was it the Ugly Sweater Run? Santa Shuffle? What was the name of that race anyway?"

"The Jingle Bell Run," I said through gritted teeth.

"It really is too bad the concert and the Elf Run are on the same day," Monica continued, ignoring my correction. She clicked her tongue sympathetically. "Funnily enough, I'm *also* training for a 5K. I haven't signed up for any particular race, yet, but it's a nice small goal to set, before I move on to something more challenging. Something like a 10K, or maybe a half-marathon." She paused. "You motivated me, Kells."

Did she say something nice? I rubbed my head to check for blood. Maybe I hit my head when I fell and was now stuck in some weird hallucination.

"Oh and thank you for those cereal crispy treats. Michael, Lindsay, and I enjoyed them that evening. That was so sweet of you," she continued.

My face grew hot. I was truly an evil queen. She bit the poisonous apple.

"Hey, Kells, are you coming?" Fiona yelled from across the parking lot.

"I have Dora the Explorer Band-Aids™ for you if you need one. All out of Cinderella and her wicked step-sisters," Georgia said, with a pointed glance I was sure Monica didn't detect. They all watched Monica; protective the way only best friends can be.

"Best of luck with your training," I choked out, and quickly backed away to join my friends, leaving her alone. *That wasn't bad now, was it?* I glanced up.

"What was that all about?" Fiona asked when I joined the group. "Was that Monica?"

"The one and only," I said, accepting the bandage from Georgia. I slapped it on my scraped knee and pulled my new, now-torn pants down over the wound.

Georgia placed her hands on her hips and in a quiet, yet controlled voice demanded, "What on this good green earth did that woman say to you, Kelly Jo? You tell me right now. Tell me everything she said. Did she upset you yet again?"

"She stood right above me and told me she mistook me for Amy's nana," I said. "And that was about it."

"What? Are you freakin' kiddin' me? That is a bunch of hooey! That woman needs to learn just to shut that pie hole of hers if she has nothing nice to say. Didn't she learn anything from her mamma?"

"She has some nerve," Shruti said.

"Really? Do I look that old?" I couldn't let it go.

"Of course, you don't, Kelly Jo. Bless her heart, that woman needs to go get her eyes checked. And pronto," Georgia said.

"You don't look anything like Amy's grandmother, Kelly Jo," Fiona added. "Look at you. You've got great, shapely legs and beautiful caramel-brown hair."

"And you're young and strong," Shruti said softly. I felt a rush of gratitude.

"Monica sure doesn't think so," I said, and glanced back up the hill. Monica jogged in the opposite direction. "I'd kill for her figure."

"Or that thick hair," Fiona said.

Georgia shot Fiona a look.

"What?" Fiona said defensively.

"Y'all need to stop comparing yourself to other women," Georgia said.

"Besides, that hair is thick because it hides devil horns."

Fiona turned to me. "You're smart, a hard worker, thoughtful—and you're an awesome friend. Look, we're all here about to start running because of you. You did this. So, let's forget that woman and her shenanigans and get to this running business. Monica will see that no grandma can hold a candle to you my dear friend." She held up her phone. "Okay, so I found a great app for us to use for our training. We have eight weeks until the race, so we need to stay organized."

I tried to focus on Fiona's words while she explained how we would use the app to map our training, but my mind kept swirling around thoughts of Monica. I tried taking in a deep breath and letting it out slowly, trying to get Monica out of my head. I hated how easily she got under my skin.

I looked back toward the parking lot where malevolent Monica had hovered over me and thought about the fall when we got all dressed up in our favorite Kentucky blue cocktail dresses and went to Keeneland together with the fraternity brothers. She looked gorgeous with her long legs and beautiful dark hair, and we both got hit on as soon as we got to the private event. She claimed, at least back then, it was all me. I was the main attraction. I sighed and started to jog in place. I needed to shake her off. *How had she changed so much? Or was it me? Was I the one who had morphed from princess to villain?*

"Hey, Kells..." Fiona waved her hand in front of my face. "Are you even listening?"

"Totally," I lied brightly, and punched a fist in the air. "Let's do this."

"I don't know," Georgia said uneasily. "This sounds like a lot, Fiona."

"We can do this, Georgia," Fiona said.

I imagined Monica bursting into a malicious and evil laugh as she raced past me at a finish line. I stepped over next to Georgia and whispered in her ear. "Oh, Georgia dear friend. We're doing this. We have to do this. I have to do this. I'm not letting Monica distract me." I punched my other fist high into the air. "We're staying the course girlfriends."

"Okay, okay, sergeant Kelly Jo. So, where're we running to? How about we run to someplace interesting, say breakfast? I could sure use some biscuits and gravy," Georgia said.

"Less talking. More running, ladies," Fiona said, unamused "And no biscuits and gravy for us, we're training." She looked at her phone, clicked the running timer, and jogged off without further discussion, ever dedicated to organization and routine.

I took off after her, and Shruti and Georgia followed.

"It's the eye of the tiger, it's the thrill of the fight. Risin' up to the challenge of our rival," I sang at the top of my lungs, but quickly broke off when I realized there was no way I could sing and run at the same time. I didn't have enough lung capacity. Besides, I couldn't remember the rest of the words.

According to the app, we were supposed to start with a five-minute warm-up walk, but Fiona interpreted that to be a crazy-fast walk. I tried to keep up with her pace. I finally caught up to her. I jogged by her side. I could hardly keep up. She was running so fast. "Hey, isn't this supposed to be a warm-up?" I asked, already out of breath and definitely warm.

"It is a warm-up. We're walking," Fiona said, and straightened her ballcap without missing a step.

I was about to protest again, but then her app beeped.

"Let's jog," a voice on the app said, and Fiona immediately took off at a faster pace.

The app alternated between "brisk walk" and "let's jog," which Fiona took to mean "run fast" and "run super-fast." At least, that's how it felt to me. I had a hunch that to an outside observer it would look as if I were moving at a snail's pace. Running was more arduous than it looked. How did people make it look so easy?

"How in heaven's name are you making this look so easy, Fi?" I huffed.

We ran along for several minutes, now in complete silence, Fiona breezing along, and the rest of us gasping for breath.

"I never realized...this road...was actually..." I said, breaking the silence, "a hill." I tightened my hands into fists and pumped my arms furiously, hoping to propel my body up our Kentucky Mount Everest, but the motion only made me more tired. "Are we back to 'brisk walk' yet?"

"Fiona, honey," Georgia said breathlessly, "isn't there a flat route in this town? You're gonna kill us on our first run with these dang hills."

"This is the route, ladies," Fiona said firmly. She wasn't even sweating and jogged along with seemingly limitless energy. "We can do this."

"I. Never. Knew. There. Were. So many. Hills. In Wilmore," I gasped in air, trying to catch my breath in between each word.

"Can we walk now?" Georgia asked.

"Just twenty more seconds," Fiona said.

"How are you not even sweating, Fi? I can feel sweat dripping between my boobs. Not to mention, I really have to go to the bathroom."

"That's truly sexy, Kells." Georgia laughed.

The app chirped, and the voice said, "Brisk walk."

"Thank you, Jesus," Georgia said, immediately slowing her pace.

I slowed my pace to match Georgia's. "My bladder is going to burst," I said, holding my side. "I really need to—"

"Kelly Jo, we just started," Shruti said, clearly irritated.

"I know, but I've been drinking water all morning," I said urgently. "I really gotta go. This bouncing up and down is making it worse."

"You really have to go? We've barely been running at all. I know you, Kells, this is a ploy," Fiona said, brows knitted together in concern.

"No, I swear it isn't. I filled up my Hydro Flask™ twice already this morning," I said. Fiona pursed her lips.

"Seriously? Kelly Jo, you mean to tell me you drank forty-eight ounces of water this morning before our run?"

"You told me to."

"Kells, I didn't tell you to drink it all before we go for our run. I said we all needed to start drinking more water. Can't you just hold it?"

"I can't, Fi. There must be something close by. I'll only be just a second." I looked around the street. I didn't know this street, or anyone who lived here. I thought about running over to this little house and knocking on the door, but then I saw a line of trees in the distance. "Hey, I can just run up that little hill. Up there." I pointed up the hill.

Horrified, Shruti placed her hands over her eyes and glanced up the hill. "That looks like a construction site. Isn't it?"

"I don't care if she goes. I support her," Georgia said.

"Of course, you do, Georgia. And Kelly Jo, that is a public site. It's out in the open."

"No worries, Fi. Look, nobody is around, *and* there are super thick bushes." I pointed at a row of shrubs along the hill. "It wouldn't be totally public. Also, aren't we supposed to stop and smell the roses along the way?"

"Honey, that's honeysuckle, which is a weed," Georgia said. "I do believe it smells good though— maybe it'll mask any other extra odors."

"Kells, just wait until we get back. We'll just be a little while longer," Fiona said.

"It will be fine. Just give me a second." I stepped away from everyone, making sure not to lock eyes with Fiona or Shruti. I lunged up the grassy hill, lined with piles of lumber. "It is an emergency. When nature calls, you gotta answer."

"I can't believe she's going to do this. Is this even legal? Is this socially acceptable?" Shruti whispered, clearly embarrassed.

"I can hear you, Shruti," I said.

Then I heard Georgia. "Yes. This is perfect. While she goes, let's take just a little sweet break."

Georgia's words faded as I got closer to the tree line. I ducked behind the row of honeysuckle and struggled to pull down my tight running pants. They were completely stuck to my sturdy, sweating legs, but I managed to get them down and then—*ahhh*. My

107

whole body relaxed. I breathed in the aroma of the honeysuckle.

"Midnight. Midnight!" A man's deep voice boomed.

I stopped breathing and tried to yank up my jogging pants, but it would be easier to put a balloon on a giant-sized pumpkin than get my pants up and over my rear end. I yanked again but felt a lick on my hand.

"What in the world?" I looked behind me and standing within inches of my back was a beautiful black lab, playfully wagging his tail. He barked cheerily.

"Midnight. Midnight!" The voice grew louder. Whoever it was, was getting closer.

"Good dog," I whispered, and yanked up my pants. The waist was all rolled over, but I was somewhat hopeful that I was covered. "*Shhhh.*"

"Um, hello."

I jumped up at the sound of his voice and my hair jumbled into the Honeysuckle. The stupid weed yanked my head, and I stumbled backwards, but the dog stepped closer, cushioned my legs, and then the most amazing thing happened. Erik Wellsworth reached out and grabbed my flailing right arm, stabilizing me at last.

"My stars!"

"Sorry, I didn't mean to scare you." He smiled a self-confident movie-star grin. Immediately, my stomach turned flip-flops and my knees started to buckle. I inwardly chastised myself, finding it unsettling that one smile had such an effect on me.

"I was trying to catch up with my dog. He raced off, but I'm so sorry I scared you. I didn't know anyone was around." He looked at me curiously, and I scrambled for a socially acceptable reason why his dog found me squatting in a honeysuckle bush by a construction site, other than to take a pee in the middle of a run.

I felt my cheeks flush. "I was just checking out this beautiful bush. This honeysuckle bush," I stammered. "I love plants." *And now he thinks I'm an idiot.*

"Kells, are you done yet? I'm gonna have to pee next if you take any longer," Georgia said from below, unable to see Erik or me. I could barely make her out through the bushes. She was sprawled on the ground, both arms draped over her eyes.

Erik's eyes sparkled with amusement.

"I was um...those are my um..." I stuttered feeling my face flush. His dog licked my hand. "You...um, I mean, your dog is adorable." This was surely a dream. I blinked and then opened my eyes slowly. He was still there.

"He likes you. I think he has pretty great instincts."

I opened my mouth to speak, but no words came to mind. Nothing. His eyes crinkled like he was holding in a laugh. His dog licked me, and I patted it on the head.

"Sorry for interrupting your honeysuckle viewing," he said lightly. "I'm actually glad that we bumped into each other again."

"Me too, Erik. Erik Wellsworth," I said drawing out his name, thankful for words to finally form and exit my mouth. "Wellsworth is such a dreamy...I mean, nice, name. Isn't it? And I'm Kelly Jo Raymond. *Miss* Kelly Jo."

He feigned seriousness, his eyes crinkling slightly at the corners, obviously amused at my unease. "A great name as well."

"KeeeelllyJooo..." Georgia yelled. "Are we gonna finish this run or what, girlfriend?"

"I think I should probably go now. We're kind of in the middle of a run," I said, and nodded to where my friends waited. "It was nice to see you again. And nice to meet you," I said to Midnight, scratching behind his soft, dark ears.

"Before you go, Miss Kelly Jo Raymond," Erik said, his cheeks now flushing slightly, "the other day when I asked if we could get coffee at your school, I really did mean it. Do you think I could get your number?"

"Yes," I said, before he could change his mind. "But I am afraid I don't have a pen on me." I patted at my tight-fitting running pants.

He pulled out his phone. "I can plug it in right now."

"Sure. Of course." I rattled out my number, all the while grinning like an idiot and hoping I was actually giving him the right number with the digits in the correct order.

"Gotta go. Team-in-training calls!" I bounded down the hill like a sprite gazelle leaping and running on the balls of my Fit. A cheetah racing across the desert. A goddess sprinting in the woods.

It was a little too much speed—I was pretty sure I wasn't going to be able to stop once I got at the bottom of the hill, and I not only hoped he wasn't watching, but I desperately hoped that at least Georgia could stop me. Otherwise, I might just keep on going.

~ Fifteen ~

"We just finished the Louisville Zoo 5K. For part of the race, we ran by the emu cage, and the emu was pacing with all of the runners as they ran by."
-Beth, runner for three years

Our first full week of training flew by. Although it had been unusually muggy for late October, none of us were deterred. Our little app—and Fiona—kept us moving.

"See you all Monday," I said. "Thanks for an awesome week. I know now I can run at least one minute."

"We can do anything for one minute. Right Kells?" Georgia cheered before she slipped into her SUV. "TFIG!"

"Yes, TGIF," I said, then walked across the parking lot, heading straight to my truck, legs wobbling like gelatin. "We can do this," I said to myself. A drop of sweat dripped off my brow, and I brushed it away. It felt good. Even the sweat.

"Kells, wait up." Fiona ran over to my truck. She started stretching with one leg, and I started to mimic her, but then she lifted an arm behind her back to stretch her arm instead of her other leg. It was weird. It wasn't like her. She suddenly stopped. "Kells, I hate to ask you because you're so busy lately, and I know you have a super-full schedule—"

"What is it, Fiona?" I kept trying to copy her stretches while we talked.

"I'm going out of town this weekend to visit my

parents again. My Dad is sick. Do you think you could run by my house and maybe walk Romeo tonight and then let him out in the morning? I know I always ask you to do this, but he likes you. And you know how finicky he is. I know you're so busy with Amelia and colleges and everything. But I promise I'll pay you back somehow."

I smiled. "Fi, no worries. First of all, you are so *not* paying me back, girlfriend. Secondly, I could totally use the extra exercise. You're practically doing *me* the favor."

"You're a gem, Kells." Fiona gave me a quick sweaty hug. "I'll be back Sunday. Thank you so much."

"No problem whatsoever."

I walked to my truck, rolled down my windows, and put in my Drake Douglas CD, spirits high.

~ * ~

That night, after Amelia left for her a cappella practice and sleepover, I threw on my UK sweatshirt and new sneakers and headed over to Fiona's house. I was happy to watch her dog—it was nice to have some small way to pay her back after what a great friend she had been to me all these years.

I'd been in the house less than a minute when I was greeted by a cotton-colored ball of energy, licking my shins and barking excitedly.

I giggled, allowing the impromptu bath. "Hey, fella, no one has to say, 'Wherefore art thou, Romeo' for you, do they?"

The bichon sat on his plump haunches, tilting his head, studying me with curious, gentle eyes. I rubbed under his chin. "Okay, no more Shakespeare. How 'bout we go for a walk?"

When I spoke the magic words, he started

spinning in circles. Fiona took him for a walk every day after school, and he absolutely loved it. He stepped through each leg hole in the harness, just like a pro. It was obvious he was well behaved.

"If you were mine, you'd probably jump all over people, or worse yet, run away." Romeo barked in response, like he could understand me.

I pulled on his harness and took him outside, looking up at the sky and the hints of red and orange as the sun was starting to set. The smell of fresh fall leaves permeated the evening air. It was a perfect October night.

I mulled over our training from the week and walked a bit straighter just thinking about what I had already accomplished. I had no idea how I would ever run a 5k, but I wasn't going to worry about that tonight. It was too beautiful. I took several steps forward before Romeo stopped to sniff something.

I stood waiting for Romeo. "Oh Romeo," I whispered. I imagined finishing the Jingle Bell Run with Drake Douglas—the Romeo of country music. We'd all be laughing as we sprinted through the finish line. Drake would ask us if we'd all like a cappuccino. At his house. We'd all gather together around his fireplace trading race stories and sipping caramel cappuccinos.

He'd ask in his sweet, deep southern voice, "Ladies, would you care to join me for another benefit run? It was amazing to run with y'all. We need to do it again. Oh, and Kelly Jo, you need to follow your other dreams, too. How about I help you get set up for those classes you need? Aw heck, I'll pay for it—and I'll pay for Amelia, too. You don't need to worry your lil' head about a thing."

Romeo tugged on the leash. I put my headphones

in and selected my favorite Drake Douglas song. Romeo pranced along, and I let myself drift off into the music

Without warning Romeo jerked the leash from my grip and sprinted away. I leapt forward trying to get my balance while simultaneously trying to jump on the leash trailing behind the dog. "Romeo. Come back, Romeo."

He raced around a corner with me in panicked pursuit. "Oh please, Romeo—don't run away from me." *Fiona is going to be devastated.* I shot up another arrow prayer, *God, I'm sorry I keep sending up these quick prayers, but I do so need your help.* I ran around the corner and came to an abrupt halt. It would have been almost comical *if* I hadn't almost landed on my best friend's pooch and *if* there wasn't the biggest, blackest dog I had ever seen in my entire life.

I gasped for breath, partially because of my sprint, partly because the dog looked very familiar. "Midnight?" I whispered. I followed Midnight's leash swaying in the air, right up to his owner. I blinked, blinded by the lantern along the path. Standing in front of me was Erik, like a star surrounded by rays of light. He looked up and smiled, the corners of his eyes wrinkling in amusement.

"Kelly Jo."

"Erik," I said, trying to grab and untangle the leashes. "We were out for a walk, and he took off, and I was so worried. I'm so sorry."

"Cute dog," he said, nodding at Romeo.

"Romeo. You're—I mean, *he's* Romeo," I stuttered

"Pardon?" he asked, smiling wider, obviously savoring my embarrassment.

My cheeks burned. Why was the guy having such an effect on me? "Romeo is the dog's name. He belongs to my friend, Fiona—I'm just walking him while she's out of town," I said.

He stepped closer, the fragrance of his cologne wafting through the evening breeze. It was mysterious, like Erik. "That's nice of you. I felt guilty leaving Midnight alone all day today—I just started our walk. Glad I bumped into you again. I think you gave me the wrong number. It bounced back when I tried to text."

"You did? You texted me?" My heart fluttered.

"Maybe it was my fault," he said. "I probably typed in the wrong number when you gave it to me on the hill."

Maybe I did. I was a little distracted trying to pull up my dang pants.

"Do you want to join us? If you're in a hurry or something, that's no problem. But I'd like to catch up and reminisce about youth group." He shifted nervously around the dogs and untangled the leashes.

"With just me?" I asked, looking around.

"No," he said smiling. "How about all four of us?" He nodded at the dogs.

Erik wanted me to walk with him? My heart raced, but this time it wasn't from being horribly out of shape while running.

"I would love to walk with you until midnight...I mean, with Midnight." I mentally beat myself up. *Don't be a dork. This isn't high school, just play it cool.*

Erik broke into his celebrity-type smile. "It's a blessing I met up with you again. The text I tried to send was an invitation to dinner. I have this restaurant I have been wanting to take you to. It has such a lovely ambiance. I imagined when I designed, I mean, I would love your opinion."

"Dinner?" I couldn't believe my ears. I stopped, and Romeo turned and looked at me, confused. "My opinion?"

This time it was Erik's turn to be flustered. "If you don't want to go for dinner, we could go for coffee," he said quickly.

"Dinner, with *me*?" I croaked.

"Yes, and I think you might like it. At least I hope you like it," Erik said eagerly.

"I would love to," I said before he could change his mind. "I would really love that, Erik." I surreptitiously pinched my arm, but he didn't disappear. This was no dream.

Erik launched into a memory from our days in high school, but I had such a hard time concentrating. I just kept looking at him and smiling like a crazed woman. I couldn't believe I was walking and talking with Erik Wellsworth. And he wanted to take me to dinner.

My legs were tired, but I didn't say a word about it. I just wanted to walk and talk with this man all night.

Romeo pranced along next to Midnight. I knew exactly how Romeo felt, happy to be walking next to a brown-eyed dream.

~ Sixteen ~

"Your overall health, both physical and mental, will be better overall if you persevere and keep running."
-Amy, runner for fifteen years

I jumped out of my truck, threw my purse strap over my shoulder, and practically skipped into Rose Will Monroe Elementary School.

"Hi, Tricia," I said and signed in on the computer. "How are you on this gorgeous October Monday morning?"

"I'm well, thank you. You look great today, Kelly Jo," Tricia said, raising a brow.

"Thank you. I feel great," I said, grinning like the Cheshire cat. "Did you see my personal request for Friday? I'm hoping to take Amelia for a college visit."

"It's ready to go. Just waiting for the principal's signature." Tricia smiled back at me. "I can't believe Amelia's a senior already. It seems like just yesterday she was graduating Rose Will and heading to middle school."

"You're telling me," I said, and deflated slightly at the thought. Time moved too fast. I needed to yell "freeze," so I could keep Amelia with me for a little longer.

"Does she know what she wants to major in?"

"I'm not really sure what she wants to do. Something with singing." My high deflated even more. "But maybe she'll figure it out during a college visit. We're off to Nashville to check out Vanderbilt this weekend. Apparently, they have a wonderful school of music and hopefully good financial aid too."

Tricia nodded approvingly. "My niece went there, and she absolutely loved it. I'll make sure Lou knows you'll be gone."

Almost on cue, Lou walked out of his office, mustache bristling as always. "Make sure I know what?" he asked gruffly.

"Kelly Jo is taking a personal day on Friday," Tricia replied tartly. "She's taking Amelia on a college visit."

Lou stared at me, deadpan. "Amelia's a senior?"

"Yes. Can you believe it? Time flies," I said twisting my bracelet around my wrist.

Lou licked his lips. "Does this mean you'll be moving on from Rose Will?" he asked, eyes still emotionless.

"Moving on?" I repeated, shaking my head in confusion.

Lou sighed, as if he were addressing one of my kindergarten students. "Will you be moving closer to wherever Amelia goes to college? Perhaps taking on a different job to help with college?"

I felt light-headed. The JoJo incident was coming back to haunt me. "No, I love it here. Do you want me to leave? Are you *asking* me to leave?" I blinked away tears. "I might not be a fully certified teacher, but I promise I'm going to get my certification someday, and when I do, I would absolutely love to teach here."

Principal Lou opened his mouth to respond, but then the phone rang.

"Rose Will Elementary School," Tricia answered,

and then paused. "Sure, he's right here. Just a moment, and I'll put him on." Tricia set the phone down on the counter and pushed a button on the pad. "Principal Lou, that was the delivery next door for the construction site. They need to talk with you about the buses this afternoon."

"Excuse me, but I have to take this," he said brusquely. He turned around and while heading toward his office I heard him declare, "but Kelly Jo, let's pick up this conversation later."

I felt as if an elephant had sat on my heart. My future at the school was becoming apparent. "I would be okay if we didn't," I whispered, and dashed out of the office.

I walked in a daze to the classroom, imagining my next job closed in a room, filing papers in a cabinet all day long. Talking to no one. Nobody. Except maybe a few mice that I named, since I would be so lonely.

"Hey, Kells." Fiona looked up from her desk when I entered the classroom. "Wow, you look really pale. Is everything okay?"

"I thought my life was finally being pulled up from the pit," I grumbled, "but I've been shoved back down with force."

"What are you talking about?"

"I ran into Lou. He asked me if I was leaving Rose Will."

"Leaving? What do you mean, leaving? Why would he ask you that?" Fiona asked, confused. "Are you leaving?"

"No. I love it here." I reached for a small chair and slumped into it. "This is probably about the JoJo incident," I said throwing my head down on the table. "Lou was furious about that. It was probably the last straw, and now he can force me out and replace me with someone younger and more competent." I lifted my head. "Someone who has certification. Someone who doesn't quit or doesn't just imagine great things for herself, but someone who actually completes stuff and isn't a loser." I threw my head back down and buried it in my arms.

"Kells," Fiona put her hand on my shoulders. "You just tell Lou to," she picked up a paper leaf off the table, "*leaf* you alone. You're great at what you do and you're never leafing."

The corny joke fell flat. I couldn't smile. I couldn't let out even a sympathetic chortle at her bad pun. My good mood had completely evaporated, and I was a total bundle of nerves and annoyance.

"Fi, what's happening?" I said, raising my head again. "I can't run this race. I have sturdy legs, a daughter who hates me, and—"

Fiona pulled out a chair and plopped down next to me. "And a group of girlfriends who adore you and think you're smart. Oh, and don't forget that totally hot guy from your youth group taking you for romantic walks because you're so interesting," Fiona interrupted. "You're getting out of this rut, Kells. You said so yourself. Don't let Lou, Monica, or anyone else, including yourself, stop you."

I sighed and plucked at a loose string on the chair. "I wish I had your life, Fiona."

Fiona shook her head and chuckled softly. "No, you don't. I'm by myself, Kells. You have Amelia. She is awesome, and talented, and sweet. I know things are tough right now, but she loves you, Kells.

"Okay, I wish I had your body. But I've got these tree trunks." I smacked my legs.

"As for those so-called sturdy legs of yours, they're beautiful. We all have stuff about ourselves we don't love, Kells. Look at me." I sat up away from the table and looked up at her. "Look at these arms. I have arms like chicken legs." She pushed up her blue long-sleeved blouse to reveal her arms. It suddenly occurred to me that she always wore long sleeves, even when it was ninety degrees outside. I never connected the dots before.

"Seriously, Fi, you don't have chicken arms."

"Yes, I do. Some girl in junior high told me, and I knew then, she was right. My arms look like scrawny, skinny chicken legs." She put her hand back on my shoulder. "The point is, we've all got stuff we're dealing with, Kelly Jo. We can't let those things stop us from accomplishing our goals and dreams. We have to simply be intentional about what we're doing and move forward."

The students poured into the room, signaling an end to our conversation.

I squeezed Fiona's hand resting on my shoulder and said softly, "First off, forget that girl in junior high, because you, my friend, have beautiful arms. Secondly, how did you get so wise for such a young whipper-snapper?"

"I try. And I'll try to love my arms, if you promise to love your legs," she whispered back.

"Deal."

I took another deep breath, managed a shaky smile and turned toward the kiddos. "Hey, friends. Happy Monday."

~ * ~

After work, Fiona showed up in a long-sleeve athletic shirt for our run. We all started our stretches.

121

"Um, I thought you were going to start, you know—forgetting those chicken arms," I whispered to Fiona.

"Okay, Miss 'I hate my sturdy legs'. Why are you in pants?" She whispered just a bit too loud.

"Rome wasn't built in a day," I exclaimed.

"What's going on?" Shruti stopped stretching. "It's seventy-five degrees. Why in the world are you wearing long sleeves, Fiona? And Kelly Jo, pants? And why are you both mumbling to each other about it?"

"Kelly Jo thinks she has sturdy legs," Fiona said.

I put my hands on my hips, resisting the impulse to stick out my tongue like a kindergartener on the playground. "Fi thinks she has chicken arms." Fiona smirked and made a face.

Shruti burst out laughing. "You both are hilarious. I thought I was the only one who was weird. Did you know I hate my hair? I wear a hat any chance I get, because I have crazy, frizzy hair."

"Awe, Shruti, I love your hair," I said. "Georgia probably doesn't have any issues. Miss Always Confident would be so disappointed in all of us." I laughed. "Where is she, anyway?"

"Georgia can't run with us today," Fiona said. "Gracie is sick, so she's staying home with her. I couldn't believe it. She was really bummed to miss out on training."

"We'll have to channel her confidence while she's gone," I said, and rolled up my pants a tiny bit. One step at a time.

We started our warm-up walk. We all stopped talking and fell into a comfortable, even pace.

"Kelly Jo, you're pretty quiet today," Shruti said, beginning a light jog.

"I feel like I'm ridin' some crazy roller coaster,

y'all. One minute I'm soaring down the track with Erik-Gorgeous-Wellsworth livin' my best life, and the next, I'm holding on for dear life whipping around a corner while Lou yells on the sideline telling me how I'm a complete and utter failure. I jumped on a random acorn, pulverizing the small nut into the pavement, pretending to crush Lou's disapproving stare from my mind.

"Lou asked if she was going to leave," Fiona said from a few paces in front of us. "To be fair, though, it wasn't totally out of the blue."

"What?" Shruti asked. "Why?"

"He wanted to know if I was leaving now that Amelia was leaving." I drew in a deep breath. "Why in the world would I be leaving? I'm not the one going to college."

"Maybe you should," Shruti said thoughtfully. "Haven't you always wanted to get your teaching certification or finish your elementary education degree? Or was it both?"

"Let's jog," the app interrupted, and we picked up the pace.

I didn't answer Shruti, partly because I was waiting for the app to tell us we could walk again, and partly because I didn't know what to say. I jogged forward, lost in my own thoughts, my legs heavy.

"How could I afford that?" I finally said, once we slowed to a walk.

"Seems like you always have some excuse," Shruti said lightly. I gritted my teeth, fighting back tears. Were my friends giving up on me now, too?

"I could have made an excuse not to train," I said, trying not to get riled up, "but here I am, training with y'all. Not to mention, I'm watching my stupid sugar intake. It seems lately I win, and then I lose."

"No, you don't. You can get your degree, too," Shruti said in that same reasonable voice, that started to sound like fingernails on a blackboard.

"You make it all sound so easy, Shruti," I said, raising my voice. "You know that things happen, and—"

Then it happened. Before I could finish my sentence, I gagged. Then I choked. I stopped and stood by the side of the road spitting. "Something. Flew. Into my mouth." I yelled in between spits.

"Let's jog," the app said. Shruti and Fiona started to jog.

"Hey, wait up. I can't. *BLECK!* I swallowed a bug y'all." I stood still choking and spitting trying to get the dang bug out.

"You're fine," Fiona said. "Spit it out or just swallow it and move on, girlfriend. We've got running to do." Both left me in the dust spitting all by myself.

~ Seventeen ~

"When traveling, I always pack my running sneakers. I won't say that I always run, but if you don't pack it, you're definitely not going to do it."
-Beth, runner for three years

I knew hotel workout rooms existed, but this was the first time in my entire life I had gone *inside* one.

I had one hour until I needed to shower and get ready for Amelia's college visit, and I had promised myself I would use that hour to work out. However, the room felt dauting–it was small, with mirrors on the walls. There was a little station equipped with a cooler, water bottles, and towels, making a cloud-like display.

I barely knew what half the machines in the room did, and I had never even been on a treadmill—something I wouldn't readily admit to anyone—but how hard could it be? Besides, I had to do it. This was Friday, and I was missing another training run with Fiona, Georgia, and Shruti. I couldn't afford to skip a workout.

"You can do this, Kelly Jo," I said under my breath, wishing I had my support group. The workout room was completely empty, probably because everyone was enjoying sleeping in and eating Belgian waffles from room service. "Don't think about waffles. Just focus."

I opened my gym bag and grabbed my sneakers, one in each hand.

"Sugar!" I had one wonderful almost new

goddess sneaker, and one stained-green lawn mowing sneaker. I rubbed my forehead. *Just great.*

"I won't let this stop me," I muttered, and shoved on my Nike™ shoe. I went to put on the lawn-mowing shoe, and then realized that not only were the sneakers mismatched—they were both *lefties*.

Still undeterred, I shoved the old roomy left sneaker onto my right foot. Okay, this could work. Sure it was awkward, but the room was empty. No one would see.

I made a beeline for the treadmill before I lost my nerve, stepped onto it, and stared at the controls. I pushed quick start. Nothing happened.

"Bless your heart, you can't operate a simple treadmill," I said to myself, feeling like an idiot. I pushed more buttons, and finally all the lights came on.

I pushed quick start again. It may have been called quick, but the treadmill belt moved at a snail's pace. I hit the increase speed button, deciding to stick to Fiona's regular training plan to walk for a minute and run for two minutes.

I placed my cellphone on the treadmill shelf in front of me, put my headphones in, and hit shuffle on my new running playlist.

In a moment of thoughtfulness, Amelia had put together a list of songs she thought would be perfect for running. Of course, she did it because apparently my music was "horrible," and I needed to "get some songs from this century." I didn't see anything wrong with my extensive Shania Twain collection, but I wasn't about to turn down some new tunes.

The belt below me moved slowly, and while I walked, my thoughts drifted to last night.

Amelia and I drove to Nashville after school and

had dinner at a local place called *Burger Up*. I was tempted by the juicy-looking burgers and stacks of fries but resisted the impulse to stuff my face. I ordered a salad instead.

Our waiter was an aspiring singer/songwriter, and Amelia was enamored. She and the waiter chatted about songs and gigs as I stole just a few of Amelia's French fries.

Even though I didn't understand the technical details of the music and didn't recognize half of the trendy places the waiter said he was playing, I had to admit that I was reminded of one thing—Amelia really was passionate about music. The way she glowed when she talked about writing songs and singing made it clear that this was what she loved to do. I felt a tiny pang of guilt. Was I wrong for insisting that she go to college? Could she really make a go of singing without higher education?

I pushed the thought away. No. I never finished anything but that didn't mean my daughter would have to fall into the same trap. She was going to go to a good school and get her degree.

The thumping music on the playlist pulled me back to the present. I glanced down to see the name of the song. *Toxic*, by Britney Spears.

Oh my, I thought, glancing toward heaven. *But you gotta admit, this song has a great beat.*

I lost myself in the music while I jogged along on the treadmill. It was a bit easier than jogging in Wilmore, even with two left sneakers on my Fit. This was working. I didn't have any stupid hills in the workout room and I even tried to dance a bit while I ran.

The next song came on. *Confident* by Demi Lovato. When she repeated the chorus, I started feeling more confident. *I could do this.*

Sweat began to drip down my chest again. I felt sweat dripping between my boobs again. It dripped down into my left eye, and I quickly wiped it away, then hit the plus button on the treadmill and sped up to match the pace of the song.

But as luck would have it, when I pushed the increase button, I held my finger down a little too long. The treadmill began to speed up, and I had to run faster and faster to keep my pace. I grabbed onto the sidebars for support, Demi's voice blasting in my ears, and I gasped for breath. I raced to keep up with the little black carpet-belt spinning around beneath my Fit. I was on the carpet ride of my life. I fumbled, trying to reduce the speed, but stumbled and grabbed the sidebars once again for balance. I couldn't let go to slow it down. Sweat dripped into my eyes, and my headphones fell out of my ears. The music cut out. I was holding on for dear life and running faster than I ever knew my sturdy legs could take me.

Flashing before my eyes, I imagined the president of Vanderbilt University standing next to my lil' machine. He'd take one look at me, and yell, "Never! Her daughter will never go to our university. She's insane. The apple doesn't fall far from the tree y'all."

I quickly wiped away the sweat and then reached over to try and reduce the speed once again. I felt a horrible scrape as my old left mowing sneaker rubbed along the side of the treadmill. Of course, it would be a *shoe* that would cause me to slip—here we go again, Cinderella.

Instead of gracefully descending some wonderful spiral staircase, wearing a blue ballgown, I flew off the back of the machine and landed on the floor in a heap. The treadmill continued to spin, bumping into my left goddess sneaker with a steady beat. My sneaker, loosened by the belt, flew off across the room. There was no prince nearby to pick it up–I was on my own. The song still played faintly out of the headphones on the floor, and the chorus now sounded mocking instead of inspirational.

I did my best impersonation of a crash dummy as I lay sprawled on the floor trying to catch my breath. A wave of relief washed over me when I saw the room was still, mercifully, empty.

Thank you, Lord, that no one witnessed that embarrassing fiasco. Gingerly, I moved each of my extremities. No obvious pain. I slowly stood. I took off my other sneaker and picked up my headphones. I held them in my hand, moving my head from my hand to the treadmill like watching a ping pong match. I reached up and stuck one headphone in, then the next. Demi Lovato's *Confident* faded into *Fight Song* by Rachel Platten. I jutted out my chin and clenched my fists. This treadmill was not going to stop me. With new resolve, (and no sneakers), I jumped back on the treadmill and pushed quick start once again. "'Cause I still got a lotta fight left in me..." I bellowed along with Rachel Platten.

I imagined Vanderbilt's President stepping into the room and noticing my socks pounding the belt. "This family of Raymond women has spunk. We need more strong women at this university. Admit her immediately!"

~ Eighteen ~

"Don't compare yourself to other people. Running is about your personal best."
—Julia, runner for nine years

I pulled into the parking lot, put my truck in park and hopped out. I glanced at my phone and noticed the date. It was already week three. I couldn't believe it was the end of our third week of training. I headed toward the field where we always met and plopped down on the grass. I was about to stretch but instead, I threw my whole body down on the ground and looked up at the sky and just relaxed. It was a beautiful day for a run. Perfect.

Today we were going to jog for three minutes and walk for three minutes—a step up from our previous routine.

A single cloud moved over and blocked the sun. I sat up and looked around to make sure Monica wasn't anywhere in sight. She would certainly bring storm clouds, and I wasn't up for any clouds today. I wanted blue skies and sun.

I noticed Georgia pulling into the parking lot with her huge white SUV. She got out and sauntered over to me.

"How did it go at Vanderbilt?" she asked immediately, sitting on the grass right next to me. "Did Amelia like it? Will she apply?"

"Maybe."

Georgia raised an eyebrow knowingly. "You're not ramblin', so something's not right. Spill."

"Thursday was perfect," I said. "Other than a small workout center fiasco. But on Friday, I took Amelia on the Vanderbilt tour, and it all fell apart."

"We'll circle back to the workout center fiasco story later," Georgia said, never one to miss a thing, "but what happened Friday?"

"We went out for lunch after the tour..." I paused.

"And what? What happened?" Georgia leaned closer.

"We met this really sweet waiter, and it turns out he wants to be a singer. He and Amelia hit it off."

"That doesn't sound horrible."

I stretched my legs and bent over slowly.

"And?" Georgia asked.

"I think that guy ruined the whole college visit. He made Amelia think all over again about this crazy idea of becoming a singer in Nashville. Amelia told me she didn't want to go to college. To any college," I said in a rush. "She told me she wanted to sing. She threw the brochure in the garbage and stomped out of the restaurant. She didn't speak to me the entire ride home."

Georgia squeezed my shoulder sympathetically.

"I'm sure Amelia will end up exactly where she's supposed to be. You know that God has plans for her, and for you."

"Yeah, well, that sounds—"

"Hey, ladies." Shruti appeared at our side. "What sounds what? Why aren't you up and stretching? Something going on?"

"No." I glared at Georgia. "Nothing is going on."

Georgia straightened, and stared at us wide-eyed. "You know, I cannot believe I'm not sore today," Georgia said.

I shook my legs out as I stood. "I'm not either."

"Don't let Fiona know, or she'll run us even longer just to make sure we *do* feel sore," Shruti said, pointing to Fiona in the distance.

"My ears are burning," Fiona said, walking up. "I heard my name."

"We're just talking about how fit you are," Georgia said quickly, giving Shruti and me a wink.

"Right," Fiona said, pursing her lips. "What are those gift bags for? Are we working our arms today?"

I glanced at Shruti, suddenly noticing that she had several shopping bags with her.

Shruti stepped a bit closer. "I was out picking up some basketball shorts for my boys, and I noticed something at the store. I thought it was absolutely perfect for you two." Shruti glanced at Fiona and me. She was bubbling over with excitement as she bit her lip to hold back the surprise and handed a brown bag with yellow ribbon to Fiona, a purple-ribbon bag to Georgia, and then a bag decorated in green to me.

"Okay, ladies. What are y'all talking about? And Shruti, you never shop," Georgia said.

"These are too adorable to open." Fiona said.

"Shruti, what did you do?" I asked.

Shruti's brown eyes cast a warm glow over all of us as she looked at Georgia. "Fiona and Kelly Jo were having this moment the other day. And I felt horrible for them. I cannot believe how mean people can be, especially women talking badly about how other women look. I wanted to do something. And I figured if Kelly Jo can order crazy pink bras online, I can do a little shopping, too."

Fiona, Georgia, and I stood in a line with rapt

attention on Shruti.

"Go ahead, open them," she said.

Fiona pulled off the yellow ribbon, dug through the yellow tissue paper and pulled out a yellow athletic T-shirt. Embroidered on the shirt was three little chickens, running. Fiona burst out laughing.

"If we're a team, we need to look like one," Shruti said. "Chicken arms and all."

Georgia's shirt was purple. I opened up my bag. In it was a matching shirt, in green.

"Thank you so much, Shruti."

Shruti smiled mischievously. "Kells, you need to look again in that bag of yours. There might be something extra."

I reached back in and pulled out a little navy skirt, with shorts attached, underneath. "Oh, they are adorable. I love them, but Shruti, you know I can't show off these tree trunks."

"Oh, no you don't, Kells. If you get a gift like that, you are most definitely wearing it. Flaunt those muscles, girlfriend," Georgia said.

Shruti turned to Fiona. "Your arms are beautiful, Fi. They're strong, just right arms, not chicken arms." She pointed at the chickens on the shirt.

"We're going to train for this race in style, ladies. Look out Drake Douglas, here come the Kentucky chicks." Georgia laughed.

Shruti picked up the tissue paper on the ground. She looked so pleased. "Can you try them on?"

"Okay, okay. But if I'm going to wear this adorable skirt and show my legs to the world and God above, Fiona has to wear her shirt," I said, clutching the clothing to my chest.

"Um. I think it's too cold today," Fiona said, obviously stalling. "Won't we need something under these shirts?"

"Oh, no way. You aren't getting out of this one," Georgia continued. "Come on." She grabbed the rest of the bags, grabbed Fiona's arm and pulled her toward the gym next to the parking lot. "We can try them on in the bathroom."

We all walked into the bathroom in the athletic center, bags, and new clothes in hand. Taking a deep breath, I went into a stall and pulled off my jogging pants. I stepped into the new skirt, tugged it up, and realized that it fit perfectly. Shruti always noted the details of everything, and it seemed she knew me well.

I stared down at my pale, stocky legs, and suddenly lost all resolve. *There's no way I can do this. I'll blind everyone with these pale glowing things. Nope. Not today.* I started to pull the shorts back down and step out of them.

"Um, I don't think I should have to wear these shorts today *and* the T-shirt," I said inside the bathroom stall.

"Oh, no you don't. You're not getting out of this. I wear the shirt, you wear the shorts. That's the deal," Fiona yelled back from her stall. "You better be steppin' out of that stall with that new little skirt on your body, Kells, or you are in deep, deep trouble.

"My legs look like thick tree trunks. Treeee trunks," I said dramatically.

"They're not tree trunks. They're strong and shapely," Georgia said firmly. "Strong, like you. Now step out and let's see you flaunt those legs of yours."

I slowly came out of the stall to the applause and whistles of my friends.

"They look really good on you," Shruti said, and Fiona whistled again.

"Why in the world have you been hiding those legs for so long?" Fiona asked.

As if in an old-fashioned western movie, the door burst open, and in walked Monica. A blast of cold air hit my exposed legs. Monica stopped suddenly, and a woman behind her nearly walked right into her.

"Oh, Kells. You're here again," Monica said, surprised.

I wished she wouldn't call me Kells. Only friends called me that.

"I'm here, and I'm dressed and ready to run." I tried to exude confidence, though it was hard in the short skirt. The outfit was out of my comfort zone— even more so than my zebra-print top and tight polka-dotted leggings.

"We're going to fly like super chicks," Georgia added, pointing at her shirt.

"Those are really cute shirts," said the woman behind Monica. "And I love that skirt." She pointed at my outfit. "Aren't they adorable?" The woman looked at Monica, who stayed awkwardly silent.

"We're off for our workout," Fiona said, cutting the tension. "Come on ladies. Remember we have that thing we have to get back for, so we have to go." Fiona shoved her athletic shirt in her gift bag and opened the door.

"Gotta run." I glanced at Monica and rushed out the door.

"Enjoy your run," the woman said cheerily after us.

"Oh, I'll see you in a few weeks for the parents' preview of the show," I added glancing once more at Monica. She stood motionless, and her eyes seemed to look longingly at me with my friends. I felt a pang of pity wash over me. I walked down the hall and tried to figure out how I was feeling. Did I feel sorry for her? I stopped just before exiting the gym. *Monica wasn't happy.* I shook my head and started jogging to catch up with my friends. I'm sure Monica was fine.

When I exited the building, I caught a reflection of my legs in the glass door, and I thought, *maybe my legs* do *look strong and shapely.*

Move over Carrie Underwood.

~ Nineteen ~

"I like to eat all of the time, which Fids into a vicious cycle—if I haven't run for a few days, I might eat a half batch of cookies! But when I'm running, it helps me make better choices."
—Bethany, runner for thirty-two years

The doctor's office was freezing cold and smelled of strong antiseptic. I tried to pretend I was anywhere else while I flipped through a magazine.

I hated waiting for the doctor, and it was unfortunate that I had to race there right after our training run. I wished I would've had time to change. I held the magazine over my legs and continued to flip the pages.

I sat there imagining the doctor telling me they discovered there was actually something terribly wrong with me. My blood work showed a new disease and they had never seen anything like it. They were calling in specialists from Louisville, that was why it was taking so long. Oh, and on top of that, they wanted me to know I had full on-set diabetes. The new diet regiment and exercise wasn't working.

I flipped through the magazine, looking for any distraction I could find. Of course all that caught my eye were the recipes—"Best Cookies of the Year, Delicious Comfort Crockpot recipes, Cheesecakes to Entertain." The list went on and on, and my mouth watered.

A nurse entered the waiting room. "Kelly Jo Raymond?"

I followed her to the scale. I bit my lip in anticipation and closed my eyes. I peeked as the nurse peered at the number.

"Looks good," she said, scribbling something on her clipboard.

"Seriously?" I stared at the scale and blinked. "Oh my heavens, it worked. It really worked."

"Excuse me?" the nurse asked.

"I'm five pounds less than I was last month—and all I've done is reduce my sugar and run a little bit. This is amazing. No sweets every day, exercise, and making better choices. You know, all that diet stuff on that paper you gave me actually worked." My cheeks flushed. "I'm sorry, I'm ramblin'."

"No worries," the nurse said with a smile. "I get it—running is my mental therapy." She took me back into the room and said cheerily, "The doctor will be right in with you after she looks over your blood work. It won't be too long. And congratulations on the running."

"Thanks." I sat and dangled my feet off the edge of the sterile white mini bed.

The room had three cute paintings on the wall with scribbles and stick figured bodies. One of the pictures in this room had a house with a huge sun beaming over the top and giant, colorful flowers lining the front door. The second had lots of people with super-long legs and big heads, sitting around water, at a pool or a beach. They looked like pictures my kindergarteners might make at Rose Will Elementary.

I slipped off the bed and stepped closer to the last picture. It looked like something Amelia would have drawn when she was making cards for me. The child in the picture had a huge grin on her face, and the mom held a paper with a huge "A+" written in red ink on the top. I stared at the picture, transfixed. It was the *mom's* paper with the A+, not the childs'. *Oh, my Heavens. This is just precious.*

The doctor opened the door and startled me out of my staring. "Hello, Kelly Jo."

She walked in and perched on the stool, and I took a seat across from her.

"I looked over your blood work," she said. "I'm not sure what you've been doing since we last met."

There was a super-long, dramatic pause. Doctors didn't usually pause unless it was bad news, right? I imagined her telling me that I would only be able to eat broth for the rest of my life, and that I would have to exercise fifteen hours a day in a tiny room filled with heavy barbells without listening to music because it would only distract me.

Sweat decorated my brow. "It's bad, isn't it?" I wiped perspiration away with the back of my hand, and asked, "I didn't do enough, did I? It wasn't enough."

"No, actually, you're doing much better."

"What? I am?" I straightened and quickly scanned the room. *She was talking to me?*

"Your blood results show that your sugar is back down in the normal range, and you're doing much better. Whatever you're doing, Kelly Jo, keep doing it. I'll see you back in six months."

"Wait, that's it? That's all?"

"Yes, I'll need to check you again, but your chart looks good." She smiled and exited.

"Yes." I danced around the room and raised both hands up in victory. *Thank you, Lord in heaven.*

I grabbed my purse off the back of the chair and glanced at the Crayola colored picture before I left the room. *A+*. *Hmmm*. I thought. *I might be due for a few more changes.*

~ Twenty ~

"Having goals for running is really helpful. I log my runs, and it keeps me motivated and accountable when I write them down. When I know my goals, I know what I'm running for."
-Annika, runner for ten years

Fiona couldn't get the kids to sit still, and it was only nine-thirty in the morning. There was something in the air—either the aroma of turkey and all the fixin's or the cold snap. The kids were susceptible to any event, any weather. I couldn't blame them—I felt a little restless myself.

I swiveled in my desk chair and thought about Erik. *What was taking so long? Would I run into him again? Would he ask me out on a real date? When would I hear from that dreamy wonder again? Ever?*

I imagined us sitting in an open field on a red-and-white-checkered picnic blanket, talking and laughing together. I would throw my head back with laughter, and he would gently place his hand over mine. We'd fall back on the blanket and look at the sky, talking about what animal shapes we noticed in the clouds, just like we were young kids.

"It's very important to look at the clouds. Right, Miss Raymond? Miss Raymond?"

I heard my name and opened my eyes to see Fiona—and the rest of the class—staring at me. JoJo giggled.

"I'm just thinking about how sometimes clouds look like animals," I said quickly.

"Do you see a chocolate lab in one?" Fiona smirked.

"Absolutely," I exclaimed. The kids laughed at me.

"Let's all look out the window," Fiona said, "and describe the shapes of the clouds."

It was bright and sunny over the school, but in the distance, dark clouds moved quickly in our direction.

JoJo waved her hand frantically in the air and pointed to the dark clouds. "Miss Smith, I think there's a problem." All the students ran to the window, crowding around to get a look.

"Friends, friends," Fiona said sternly. She clapped her hands loudly, and even I snapped to attention. The students echoed their clap in response. "Students, let's all return to our seats."

"My gramma had a huge storm take the roof right off her house, and she told me that her dog almost flew away in the wind, too," JoJo yelled. "Are we gonna fly away in the wind, Miss Raymond?"

All the kids started talking, and one little girl started to cry.

"That's stupid," Leo said. "That's the story of *The Wizard of Oz*."

"It's true," JoJo insisted. "She had to get in the bathtub and put on a bike helmet and everything, and she almost forgot her dog."

The students screamed as the lights in the room flickered.

Fiona tried to direct their attention to a big calendar near the front of the room. "We're done looking out the window at the clouds," Fiona said quickly. "Let's return to a level zero volume and go back to our rug for calendar time."

Each day during calendar time, Fiona would add a new shape of the day. The kids had to guess the pattern. Usually it was one of their favorite activities, but today they were distracted by the dark clouds that enveloped the sky.

"Miss Smith, I think I know the pattern," I said over the noise, and a few kids looked away from the window and looked at me. JoJo giggled.

"You said we always know the patterns before you," Leo said.

"I think I know it to-daaay," I sang.

"How can you know it? We only have two shapes," Leo said.

The kids all stared at the calendar, their attention now on the shapes instead of the impending storm. Fiona smiled at me. We really were a great team.

"If y'all sit down crisscross applesauce and catch bubbles, I'll let you in on what I think the pattern will be this month," I directed, and they quickly shuffled into their spots, sat up straight on the carpet, and caught bubbles in their mouths—which meant that they puffed out their cheeks and, thankfully, fell silent.

"Miss Raymond, your class is so attentive," Principal Lou said from the doorway. I jumped. I had no idea he had been standing there, observing me with the students. He smiled at the kids, turned, and disappeared down the hall.

"Nice one, Kells." Fiona mouthed.

"So, what's the pattern?" Leo broke his bubble to ask, and I bit my lip.

I had no idea what the pattern was for the month. Fiona was in charge of the calendar, and my talent wasn't problem solving. At least that's what I used to think.

"The first day it was a shape with three sides. A triangle," I stalled.

JoJo frantically raised her hand in the air. Fiona called on her.

"I know. The first day was a triangle, with three sides, and the second day was a square, with four sides. Will tomorrow be a shape with five sides?"

"Very great hypothesis, JoJo," Fiona said, and I let out a relieved breath, thankful for the kindergartener to my rescue.

"That's exactly what I was going to say."

The kids all started to laugh, the gloom and doom now completely forgotten.

We continued with the morning routine. I pulled the shades down on the windows, to keep the students focused on the work at hand. Fiona played classical music, probably banking on that to have a calming effect, and the kids started their reading time.

I challenged them to read for at least twelve minutes today rather than our normal ten, and the kids quickly grabbed their picture books, got set up on the computers to listen to audio recordings, or grabbed their beginning reader books. They settled into various spots around the room, under desks, sprawled across the carpet, and in groups with stuffed animals and books.

Taylor sat alone in the reading corner with the stuffed animals, arms folded around a stuffed bear, looking like she might cry at any second. She had a book in her lap, but she hadn't turned one page. She was probably used to snow, since she was from New York, but tornados were a whole other ball game.

I grabbed my running magazine and walked over to her side. "May I sit here?"

Her lips curved slightly, and she nodded her head up and down.

JoJo followed me and plopped down directly behind Taylor.

Both Fiona and I modeled silent reading during this time, and the kids loved it that we read right alongside them. It was hard not to grade or prepare for another center on the computer during this time, but I knew that if the kids saw us reading, they would follow suit. I heard a few nervous mumbles.

"Hey friends, this is sustained silent reading," Fiona reminded everyone. "Let's be considerate and stay quiet."

We were about four minutes into our reading when Taylor tapped my shoulder.

"JoJo won't stop talking. I just want to read, Miss Raymond, and she's bothering me," she whispered.

I looked back at JoJo.

"Miss Raymond, I'm not doin' nothin'. I'm just readin'," she said. She started wiggling her legs up and down on the floor.

"JoJo, this is time to read," I said sternly.

She sighed. "But Miss Raymond, my feet feel like moving, and I can't keep them quiet. I want to be free like a unicorn and ride around with my friends."

Me too, only with a handsome cowboy, I thought fleetingly.

"I know it's hard. How about we take a quick walk around the hall and then come right back? Maybe that would get all of the wiggles out of your Fit and help you to focus on your reading."

"I knew you'd help me, Miss Raymond," JoJo said, and she jumped to her Fit. "Let's go ride a unicorn."

I looked over at Taylor, who was sitting in a corner by herself. She held a book about horses.

Horses. Unicorns. Why hadn't I thought of this before?

"Taylor, why don't you come with us?" I said, and Taylor stared at me.

"Okay," she said hesitantly, and set aside her book.

I took each of them by a hand and led them out into the hall.

"Taylor loves horses," I told JoJo. "They're kind of like unicorns, aren't they?"

"Unicorns are magic," JoJo said. "That's what I was trying to tell Taylor. I know a story about unicorns. I think she might like it."

"What is it?" Taylor asked shyly, and JoJo launched into a crazy story about a pink unicorn flying over rainbows. Taylor actually smiled as JoJo talked, and even chimed in to add some of her own details.

I felt a rush of pride as the two girls giggled and talked about unicorns and rainbows as we walked down the hallway.

Sirens suddenly pierced through the hallway, popping my thoughts. Taylor and JoJo screamed.

"It's okay. It's only a tornado drill," I told them, trying to keep my voice calm.

JoJo kept screaming. Taylor dropped my hand and grabbed JoJo's hand. "We need to find a bathtub!"

Maybe it wasn't such a good idea to introduce the two of them after all.

"Yes. And we need to make sure all the unicorns come with us. Let's go," JoJo said, and started pulling Taylor with her down the hallway and around the corner before I even had a second to think.

"No!" I took off running after them.

How had I managed to lose two kids this time? I wove in and out of kids exiting their classrooms in straight, quiet lines.

"Taylor. JoJo. Wait. Don't panic. No running," I sternly yelled as kids were coming out of their classrooms glaring at me. I slowed my jog to a brisk walk.

Unable to believe that this was happening yet again, I dashed around the corner and headed for the cafeteria. I couldn't imagine what Principal Lou would do this time. I shook my head, making sure not to imagine anything, turned the corner, and began to run. I ran inside the kitchen and nearly collided with several of the cooks heading out.

"Sorry," I said breathlessly.

I heard some random noises still coming from inside the kitchen near the pots and pans. I raced in, and sure enough, JoJo was in the middle of the kitchen, sitting on top of a large upside-down pan, with a brownie already in her mouth. She handed one to Taylor.

I grabbed JoJo's hand, which was gooey from the chocolate. I knelt down beside her and spoke in a firm voice. "JoJo, this is serious right now. We'll deal with these running Fit of yours later, but right now we have to get to the gym."

"But I was just wooking for a fub," she mumbled with her mouth full of brownie.

"Yeah, we were looking for a tub," Taylor said, holding her brownie.

"Funny how you two went to the cafeteria to look for a tub," I said, trying to stay stern, but

147

unable to keep my lips from twitching into a suppressed smile.

Principal Lou suddenly appeared at my side, and I froze, anticipating a reprimand. I stood and gripped both Taylor and JoJo's hands.

"Miss Raymond, thank you so much for your service and for your attention to these two friends," Principal Lou said, giving me an approving glance. "JoJo and Taylor, you need to do everything Miss Raymond says. This is serious, and we all need to get to the gym."

"Yesh shir," JoJo said, mouth still full of brownie. Taylor nodded, her mouth now also full.

I let out a huge sigh of relief. That was close. "Okay, friends, let's pretend we're on a secret mission," I leaned down and whispered to the two of them. "We're horses going to rescue everyone, and if we don't make it to the gym fast, no one will be rescued."

"And no one will ever get to eat brownies ever, ever again if we don't save them," JoJo said.

"Because the cafeteria ladies think that making brownies causes storms. So, let's go."

After I said it, I realized it didn't make any sense, but it did the trick anyway. A serious look washed over Taylor and JoJo's faces, and they quietly and quickly let me lead them straight to the gym. They were both fully committed to our new mission.

~ * ~

The clock struck three, and Fiona and I both breathed a sigh of relief. The day was finally over, and we made it through with no storm, no injuries, and no missing kids—despite the close call.

"It looks like it's going to clear up," I said to

Fiona. The kids were headed home, and I straightened a stack of papers on my desk. "I guess it was a paper tiger, and we'll get to run after all."

"I wasn't sure you were still going to want to run, after chasing JoJo and Taylor halfway around the school," Fiona chuckled. "I heard Taylor ask her mom if she could have JoJo over to play horses and unicorns. Nice job. I never would've thought the quietest student and the loudest would end up such fast friends."

"People can surprise you," I said. "But I *do* need to run, not only to train, but to lower my blood pressure after that fiasco."

"By the way, Principal Lou stopped by when you took the kids for their bathroom break," Fiona said, running an eraser over the whiteboard. "He asked if you would stop by his office before you leave today."

I froze. "He did? What does he want? Is he going to fire me, right before Christmas?"

"I'm sure it's nothing, Kells," Fiona said soothingly. "You're amazing, and everyone here knows it. Today was proof."

"I hope you're right." I packed up my bag and headed for the door. "Hopefully I'll see you today, unless Lou fires me, and then I won't have the energy to run."

"Kells, seriously, it'll be fine," Fiona called after me, but her words weren't reassuring. I walked to Principal Lou's office, stomach lurching with each step.

"Thanks for stopping by my office, Kelly Jo. Have a seat." He motioned for me to sit in the wooden chair across from his desk. I slipped into the chair. He felt taller somehow when he sat down in his big leather chair behind his desk. "I've been meaning to talk with you ever since you mentioned that Amelia was leaving." Principal Lou sounded formal, yet he took off his glasses and he gently folded them and placed them on his desk.

My hands were shaking in my lap. I wanted to pull a JoJo and bolt out of there, but I forced myself to stay seated and shoved my hands in my pockets.

"Fiona is an amazing teacher," I said quickly, my mouth dry. "I love working in the classroom with her." I tried to stop my legs from bouncing and jiggled them ever so slightly.

"I'll cut right to the chase," Principal Lou said. I held my breath and imagined shoving a brownie in his mouth and him standing in front of me mumbling words I couldn't hear.

"You mentioned you're close to getting your elementary certification, and you were interested in finishing your degree. Is that true?"

I nodded my head slowly. No brownie. I could hear him.

"Fiona and the rest of the primary teachers said you're excellent at what you do," Principal Lou went on. "Did you know we have a full-time position open this January? Lisa is retiring."

"I didn't know that." I abruptly stopped bouncing my legs.

"We'll miss her—she's an excellent teacher. But I think you would be a great candidate for her position. You have been with us a long time, and I think you are most definitely ready to have your own classroom. I would like to grant you emergency certification, if you would consider taking the job. You could complete your certification—the county offers college assistance to our staff."

"What are you saying?"

Principal Lou played with his glasses on his desk. "Kelly Jo Raymond, I want you on the Rose Will staff, full-time."

My mouth dropped open. I sat, stunned. I couldn't have imagined a better scenario.

After a moment of silence, Principal Lou spoke again. "I'm sorry. Maybe this isn't something you're interested in—"

"Principal Lou, I'd absolutely love to teach full time here," I interrupted, finally finding my voice. "I've been dreaming of this for years."

He broke into a huge and rare smile, pushed back his leather chair, and stood up. "Excellent. We can issue emergency certification for up to a year, and here at Rose Will, we pay for half your tuition for any grade B and above. I know that isn't perfect, but—"

I jumped up out of my chair. "That's amazing. I could take a class this spring, and then this summer I could finish."

I blurted out the dreams I had composed over and over in my head throughout the years. But this time, they were more than just dreams—they were plans. And I knew I could complete them, just like the training for my race. Walk a little, run a little.

"If you're able to complete your classes, and everything works out with your certification, I would be happy to offer you the position as a full-time classroom teacher," Principal Lou said, reaching out to shake my hand.

"Thank you so much." I shook his hand a little too vigorously. He stepped back, and I saw a slight smile on his face start to form.

"May I have a couple of days to see about starting classes in the spring, getting my schedule set, and then get back to you?"

"Take the rest of the week," he said. "We have time to fill this springtime position if you do not want it, but I do know you would be a great fit with the team."

I reached out and shook his hand enthusiastically again. "Thank you, again, for thinking of me."

I felt my chest 'splode with happiness. It seemed I didn't need a fairy godmother after all.

~ Twenty-One ~

"While I was running my leg of the Bourbon Chase, I called my husband in the middle of the night. I had him on speaker phone, because dogs were barking all around me, and it was dark. I made him stay on the phone with me, just in case a dog came out to bite me!"
-Tanya, runner for twenty-two years

It was a rare warm day for fall. My tiger-striped sweats would be super-hot (not the "hot mama" hot but the "I-am-going-to pass-out-hot"). I bit my lip and pulled on the skirt Shruti had bought me and then checked out my legs in my bathroom mirror.

"Ugh." I pointed my toe and tried to make my sturdy legs look more delicate. Nope. I heard once that when women look at themselves they think negative thoughts.

"Okay, Kelly Jo." I put my hands on my hips. "Say something nice about your legs," I said, resting my gaze on my knees.

"You have nice knees," I said to my reflection. "Gorgeous knees. In all the land, you are the woman with the fairest knees of all."

I felt slightly empowered by my new little exercise and decided that the skirt would work after all. I raced out of my bathroom, down the stairs, and belted, "Set your soles on fire. Blaze ahead at full speed. Keep your faith alive as you're running to your dreams..."

~ * ~

Shruti arrived late to our designated meeting spot, locked in an intense conversation on her cell.

Georgia, Fiona, and I continued stretching and gave Shruti her privacy. "I'll be right there," she mouthed to us, and then went back to her conversation. She looked serious.

The humidity and heat felt like July instead of the beginning of November. Kentucky weather was unpredictable. I wondered if it would be this warm during the Jingle Bell Run. In my mind, I imagined it lightly snowing, the flakes dusting my eyelashes, and me delicately twirling across the finish line like the Sugar Plum Fairy.

Shruti jogged over. "So sorry I made you wait." My visions of sugar plum fairies dancing vanished as I took in her appearance. Shruti's complexion was blotchy, and her eyes were red-rimmed, evidence of her crying.

Fiona glanced up at the sky, watching dark clouds move swiftly in our direction. "No worries."

"Are you okay?" I asked Shruti. "Are the boys okay? Everything okay at home?"

"Boys are okay. Everything is fine," Shruti said, shoulders slumping. "It's just that my husband wants to get the kids a dog. My coworker's dog just had a litter of golden doodles, and Sai thinks we should buy one. I'm not sure. Dogs are so much money, and I've never had a pet before in my life. But if we don't get one, I'm the horrible parent." She let out a long sigh.

"Dogs are very expensive," Georgia said, "but they're great pets. We want to get Gracie a dog, once she's old enough."

I raised an eyebrow and studied my distraught friend. There had to be more to the story. "Can you still run, or do you think you want to call him back?"

"It's fine. I'll talk with him tomorrow, after I do some dog research." Shruti spoke with bright, fake enthusiasm, but added, "I really need this run today."

"Let's go, then," Fiona said.

We all knew that Shruti was reserved, and she would need some space. I was surprised she had even told us as much as she did—it was a testament to our developing friendships.

Fiona hit the timer for six minutes, and we jogged in silence down the hill. Shruti ran several yards in front. Georgia and Fiona chatted animatedly, and I listened, glad to be back in a rhythm.

About twenty minutes into the run, we turned the corner on Park Street. Suddenly, a small, mangy dog raced out from under a fence. It was like watching a horror movie as the mutt scurried after Shruti. My mouth felt drier than cotton as I struggled to screech, "Watch out!"

The warning came too late, and I watched helplessly as the dog lunged at Shruti. Shruti's agonized screams spurred me on faster. My thoughts of Shruti losing her leg kept time with the slapping of my sneakers on the pavement.

I reached her side in a matter of seconds. Glancing around, I couldn't find anything. In a split second I yanked off my shirt and started waving it at the dog. I twisted it up and tried to snap at him to scare him. I yelled over and over, "Go home!"

As abruptly as it began, the dog's attack ended. It ran up the street, pausing once to snarl and bark, as if asserting dominance.

Shruti lay crumpled on the ground, grabbing the

back of her leg. My stomach heaved at the sight of her. There was so much blood.

Georgia ran her fingers through her hair and paced nervously. "We have to find that dog. What if he has rabies?"

Great, I didn't think about that. "Georgia, you stay with Shruti. Fiona, call the ambulance," I said, taking charge. "I'll find that blasted dog!" I sprinted off, pulling my shirt back on as I ran.

Lord, please help Shruti. And help me find that dang dog. I should have sent Fiona, I thought as I jogged faster, realizing I would soon run out of every ounce of energy.

Though the animal had a head start, I could see it running a short distance ahead of me toward the student center at Asbury University. I was gasping for air, but I refused to give up.

I continued around to the back of the student center, but the dog had vanished. I'd lost him, just like JoJo, and just like Monica. I couldn't hold on to anything.

"Did anyone see a little white dog with a brown spot on his back?" I looked in all directions, desperately hoping that someone would respond. Silence. *So much for the greatness of humanity.*

I ran in circles all around the student center until I finally gave up and returned to the group, just as it started to sprinkle rain.

Shruti sat on the grass with Georgia next to her. Georgia pressed a sock on the back of Shruti's leg, putting pressure on the bite.

"Did you call 9-1-1? Where are the paramedics?" I asked Georgia.

"I asked her not to," Shruti cut in. "I'll be fine. This is just... I can't believe I was just talking with my husband. This must be bad karma..." She stopped talking as the scattered showers turned to steady raindrops falling simultaneously on Shruti's face with her salty tears.

"Fiona went to get my van," Georgia choked out tearfully.

"I'll take her to the emergency room," I said. "Amelia has a cappella practice on Wednesdays, so I'm totally free."

"That would actually be great, Kelly Jo," Shruti said, teeth clenched in pain. "If you could drop me off—"

"I'm staying with you," I said firmly.

Finally, Fiona pulled up next to the sidewalk with Georgia's SUV. We helped Shruti into the vehicle, and I caught a quick glimpse of the bite. That little dog had done a lot of damage. She wasn't going to be training or running a 5K for a long, long while.

~ Twenty-Two ~

"I was running with two girlfriends through a public park to get to a trail. My friend was recently engaged and wore a gorgeous big diamond ring. As we were running, she tripped and fell. She was fine, but her knee was bleeding. It took her a few seconds to get up. An older woman at the park came over, and without acknowledging my friend's bloody knee, asked with serious concern, 'Is your ring okay?' She must have seen those sparkles from afar."
-Laura, runner for ten years

"Set your soles on fire. Blaze ahead at full speed."

My new ringtone blasted from my phone, and I answered quickly.

"Shruti—bless your heart, how are you doing? How's your leg?"

"Not so great." Her voice sounded tired, and I felt a pang of sympathy. "No one could find that stupid little dog," she continued, "and that means I have to get shots for *rabies,* of all things."

"What? That's horrible." I felt a pang of guilt. If only I had been slightly faster, maybe I could have caught up with the little vicious pup.

"Mom, what's wrong?" Amelia called from upstairs. *That girl has ears like an elephant when she wants to hear something,* I thought. *Oh, but when it is time to do the dishes, she suddenly has the hearing of my Great-Grandma Tillie.*

"Nothing, Amelia."

158

"What?" Shruti asked, confused.

"Sorry, Amelia was trying to talk to me from upstairs. I'm so sorry about the shots. Do they hurt?" I shuddered at the thought of a yardstick-sized needle going in one side of her arm and out the other.

"The first one was pretty horrible," Shruti said. "I have to have three more. Plus, the back of my leg was mangled, and I had to have twenty-four stitches." She paused, drawing in a shaky breath before continuing. "That one bite managed to stop any dreams I may have had about running this Christmas benefit 5K with all of you. After all this, I'm not very excited about getting the boys a puppy for Christmas. And I wasn't excited before. Do you know I was bitten when I was in India? Almost the same thing happened."

"Oh Shruti, that is horrible. No wonder you're hesitant about getting a dog." My stomach felt sick. "I am so, so sorry. No one ever warned us about steering clear of potentially infected dogs when jogging, but apparently, they should have." I imagined posting huge wanted signs around Wilmore with a picture of that horrible dog. Maybe I would have Amelia draw a picture of what we remembered the dog looked like.

Shruti sounded miserable. "My doctor said I can't exercise until I'm done with my shots and the leg heals. Kelly Jo, I'm so sorry to let you down for the run and the concert. Will they still let you participate with just three people?"

"Don't you worry about the concert for one little minute," I said firmly. "You just rest and get better. We only have to have three runners to participate, so we'll be fine, but we'll miss you."

"Thank you," Shruti said, relieved. "So, is it true you really took off your shirt to try and save me?" Her voice sounding lighter.

"*Ummm*, where on earth did you hear that crazy story? Oh, guess what?" I asked, changing the subject. "I made vegetarian lasagna yesterday, and Amelia didn't eat it. She said she's too stressed about college applications. How about I bring some over tonight?"

Shruti let out a simple laugh. "Kelly Jo, you are an amazing friend. You know, you don't have to do that—you have enough on your plate."

"No arguments, Shruti. I'll be over about four-thirty, and I will do anything else you need. I can clean the bathrooms, do the dishes, you name it." I ended the call, feeling a mix of guilt and sympathy. I walked over to the staircase.

"Amelia, would you unload the dishwasher, please?" I yelled. No response. She was back to Great-Grandma-Tillie hearing. "Amelia, would you please come down here for one minute?" I raised my voice louder with each word.

"Mom. I'm busy," Amelia yelled back through her closed door, music blasting in the background.

I grabbed my cell phone and texted her.

"Get downstairs. Now. Please."

"Fine," she texted back.

The music from upstairs went silent. Something clunked.

"SHH—"

"Watch your language, young lady," I inter-rupted, hands on my hips.

"I bashed my hand on the door, Mom. It hurt," Amelia said, throwing open her door. "And yelling 'sugar' doesn't help."

"Yelling swear words isn't going to help, either."
I paused, walked up a few stairs, and softened my
tone. "Is your hand okay?"

"I'm fine. What do you want?" She remained at
the top, still not coming down.

"Please come down and unload the dishwasher."

"I'm not sure how I'll have time for that, since
you want me to fill in all these stupid college
applications. I don't even want to go anyway. *You*
didn't go. This is so a double standard."

"We're not going there, missy," I said firmly.
"You know perfectly well I did—"

"I hate everything, and I'm super stressed about
all this application sh—stuff," Amelia said, clenching
her jaw.

"Oookay...never mind." I turned and walked
down the three stairs. "Obviously I need to end this
conversation, but I sure do want to tell you, young
lady, my two cents about college," I mumbled.

"Mooomma, I can hear you."

My entire body tensed, I turned and walked back
up the stairs and walked right to her door. "Amelia, I
need you to unload the dishwasher. It won't take
long. Please come down, now."

"I'll do it later. When my hand feels better,"
Amelia said and closed her door.

I leaned down and pressed my face close to the
keyhole. "I need you to do it before your a cappella
practice."

"I'm not going to practice tonight."

"What?"

Amelia threw open her door. "I'm. Not. Going."
Her voice cracked on the last word.

"Honey, I'm confused. You never skip practice." I
softly touched her hand resting on the doorknob. You

love singing."

Her shoulders slumped, and she threw herself on her bed. "I'm quitting. Why do you care, anyway? You don't want me to sing. You hate Monica, and you want to follow your dreams, but I can't follow mine. That about sums it up." And she pulled her stuffed dog over her eyes.

I stepped in quietly and sat on the edge of her bed.

Surely I had heard wrong. Was I the one with hearing like Great Grandma Tillie?

"Do you want me to talk to Monica about—" I started, but Amelia cut in.

"No, Mom. Don't talk to anyone. It'll make everything worse."

I couldn't believe it. She had let me into her room, and I was sitting on her bed. This was nothing short of a miracle.

"So, what's going on?" I said slowly, desperate not to screw this up. The less I talked, the better. *Help me to really listen this time and know what to say*, I prayed silently.

"Yesterday, Monica gave Lindsay the lead solo, even though everyone said I did it the best," Amelia said miserably. "Monica keeps telling me how good I am, and that I could sing for a career, but then she does this? I don't get her."

"I really don't get her eith—" I stopped myself. I needed to make this about Amelia, not me. "I thought all seniors were guaranteed solos in the concert," I said slowly.

Amelia threw her dog off her eyes, sat up, and pulled her knees to her chest. "Yeah, Mom. But some solos are like two lines long or duet solos. Other solos are entire songs. And Lindsay got two solos, which are both entire verses. Meanwhile *I* got one lousy line in *'O Holy Night'* for the Holiday-not-so-Spectacular-for-me concert."

"That's not right," I said, and she sighed.

"That is what happened, Momma. And then Monica said she'd give me a bigger solo for the spring concert, since you're not going to be there for the Holiday Spectacular, anyway, and someone who has family coming this time ought to have the parts."

"Monica said that? Those exact words?" I tried to remain calm, but I could practically feel my blood boiling.

"Yes, Momma. I'm not makin' this sh—" I looked at her crossly. "—*Stuff* up."

"Of all the low-down, rotten..." I stood and started to pace. I was so mad I could spit. As usual, Monica had to interfere and mess everything up. I clenched my teeth to keep my mouth shut, trying to "catch a bubble" and stay quiet, because if I started going off, I might never stop.

The only problem is that I felt as if I was the bubble, getting thinner and thinner, and Monica, with her perfect-pink manicured fingernails was reaching out and trying her best to make me pop.

~ * ~

Georgia and Fiona pulled into the parking lot at the same time. It was weird without Shruti. I felt a huge knot in the pit of my stomach.

"Ready to run, Kells?" Fiona yelled from her car.

I cracked my knuckles and shook my arms. "I'm fueled to run today. Fueled with anger."

"What did Monica do?" Fiona asked. She knew me well.

I filled Fiona and Georgia in on the latest.

"And all this is after the dress fiasco," I added. "Remember, last spring Monica told some girls that they would have to wear long-sleeved dresses because some of the girls' arms 'needed toning.'"

"Why in the world would she tell that to a young woman?" Georgia shook her head. "We need to help young women feel confident, not make horrible comments about them. Just the other day someone told me that Gracie was acting like a 'short boss' in her classroom. I said, short boss? More like little leader, missy."

"Oh, that woman is a snake. No wonder we all have issues." Fiona threw her hands up in the air. "With comments like that, it's no surprise Amelia is upset. I'd be upset. I am upset."

I noticed she clutched something small and pink when she threw up her hands. "Fiona, what in the world is in your hand?"

"Mace," Fiona said through gritted teeth. "We have to be prepared in case that mangy mutt shows up again. There's no way any dog in this neighborhood is going to hurt any more of my friends." A mischievous gleam entered her eyes. "Come to think of it, maybe we ought to try it out on Monica."

"Fiona!" Georgia and I echoed in unison.

"We're not going to be stopped from our training by any crazy mutts," Fiona said assuredly. "And while we're training today, we're going to have to plan what we're going to do about this Holiday Spectacular mess. Monica needs to be stopped."

"Fiona, you're brilliant," I said. Forget fairy godmothers and dogs named Toto—the true companions were besties.

~ * ~

"Kells, you're running way faster than normal," Georgia said, pumping her arms as she tried to keep up. "Since when did you get so sporty? And how can we talk about Monica if we're all out of breath?"

"Since I had a reason to run out all my anger," I huffed. "If I run the race, then Amelia doesn't get a solo for her Holiday Spectacular. If I don't run it, once again, I'm not finishing what I started. I'm in a lose-lose situation."

"What can we do to make it win-win?" Fiona asked, ever the problem solver.

"I don't know. Amelia still won't talk to me...at all." I took in a deep breath and inhaled a horrific smell.

"*Ahh!*" I screamed, and pushed Fiona into the ditch, seconds before she stepped on a bloated possum, rotting on the side of the road.

"Don't look," I said, and gasped in a quick breath and closed my mouth. I pulled her forward.

"Oh, gross!" Georgia screamed, and threw her hand over her mouth, gagging.

"I told you not to look," I said.

"You pointed right at it, Kells. Of course, I looked right where you pointed."

"Brisk walk," our app interrupted.

"Nope. I don't think so," Fiona said, and took off running, away from the possum and the lingering smell. Georgia and I followed, laughing and pinching our noses.

"Hold on," Georgia said when we were finally out of range of the stench, "I've got a stone in my shoe."

We stopped and waited for Georgia to take off her shoes and shake out the stone.

"I wish you could just take out the stones in my life, and then everything would be fine," I said with a deep sigh. "And the gems I want in my life—like Erik—where are they? It's been days and days and days since I've heard from him. I guess I can't blame him if he doesn't want all this." I gestured to my sweating, worn-out body.

"Kelly Jo, where's your faith?" Georgia said sternly. "You know it's all going to work out. Let's shoot up more of those lil' arrow prayers."

I hoped it would work out. *Something* had to. But my arrows felt like they were just falling to the ground.

~ Twenty-Three ~

"I always like to stop and pick a few flowers when I'm running and put them in my hair. Sometimes I run with two bouquets, one in each hand to take back to my room. It doesn't ruin your run to stop for a second and enjoy the time outside."
–Annika, runner for ten years

Our kindergarten students were all huddled on the carpet at the front of the room sitting crisscross applesauce. All of Laura Joffe Numeroff's books were lined up on the ledge of the whiteboard. Fiona stood in front of the students and held one book in her hands, but she only allowed the back of the book to show. I was at the kidney table in the back of the room getting their writing papers ready.

"Do y'all remember what book I read yesterday for our story time?"

JoJo and Taylor shot up their hands. Leo sat up straight but kept his hands in his basket. His face beamed. I could tell he knew. He couldn't contain his excitement. "If you give…"

Fiona interrupted, "Let's raise our hands." She waited. "Andy, do you know?" she asked. He beamed and shook his head. "Would you like to share with the class what it was?" He shook his head again. "Out loud?" Fiona patiently continued.

"If you Give a Mouse a Cookie," he said.

"Yes, kiss your brain, Andy." He puckered his lips and smacked his hand before whacking himself on the head. The entire class roared with laughter. "Okay, okay, class...one, two, three, eyes on me."

They all repeated, "One, two, three, eyes on you." And looked at Fiona.

"Today we're going to work on writing our own books, just like Ms. Numeroff. First, I'm going to read the book to you again, and this time I want you to listen for patterns in her story."

Fiona read the book, stopping every now and then to ask questions, and to reread certain sentences for emphasis. I could only hear Fiona reading and the clock ticking on the wall. The kids were captivated. She then talked to them about the story, and they shared what patterns they heard.

I noticed JoJo wasn't moving. She was sitting up straight, leaning toward Fiona, and following every movement she made.

"Miss Raymond has a writing prompt she is going to hand out, and I want you to work with a partner. Or if you would like, you may write your own story. We're going to start with the sentence, 'If you give a _____ a _____, then _____ is going to _____.'"

Fiona walked over to the Elmo, the little red projector, and placed the writing prompt under the Elmo. She turned it on, and the writing organizer appeared on the white board in front of the class. "I want you all to be thinking how you could use this pattern to make your very own stories. When we're done, we'll share them with each other. Again, you may work with a partner, but you can also work alone. And what do you do if you don't know how to spell a word here on our very first draft?"

Again, Taylor shot up her hand, but this time JoJo yelled out, "Just do your best."

"That's right, JoJo, but remember, we're

supposed to raise our hand."

"It's just that I can't wait, Miss Smith. I have so many ideas all jumbled in my head."

I handed out the writing prompts. Some of the students worked with partners, but JoJo went straight for her own desk. She gritted her teeth and frantically started to write. She pushed her pencil so hard the whole pencil snapped in half.

I walked over and handed her a sharpened pencil.

"Oh Miss Raymond, I am so excited."

"I know you are. Do you want to tell me what you're going to write?"

Taylor scooted her chair closer to both of us. Doug stepped over and stood next to me.

"Yes, Miss Raymond," she said, holding up her pencil. "My story will be called, *If You Microwave a Gerbil*, by JoJo."

"I like that title," Taylor said, pulling her chair even closer. Doug started to giggle behind me.

"That title does catch my attention, JoJo," I said, feeling a little queasy but not wanting to quash her creativity. "

It's really funny," Doug said.

"It is?" JoJo cheered. "That's what I wanted."

"Let's hear the rest, JoJo. Would you like me to write it for you as you tell me?" I asked.

"Oh Miss Raymond, I would love that. I can't write as fast as the words are coming out of my head."

More friends circled around us at the desk.

She stood up and cleared her throat. "If You Microwave a Gerbil, by JoJo. If you microwave a gerbil, it will surely...it will surely splat. If you microwave a gerbil, who'll lick it up? Your cat." She paused and looked at my face. "But you can't do that," she continued. "That's bad for your gerbil, and bad for your cat." She paused and wrinkled her nose and tapped a finger on her cheek. "Plus, that would be mean. So, don't put him in the machine. Give him a bath instead. And then stick him on your head."

For what felt like several seconds no one said anything, and then both Fiona and I burst out laughing. The kids joined in with us.

"That is so funny," Taylor said, smiling at JoJo.

"JoJo, I didn't know you were so funny," Doug added.

"You know, JoJo, you're a great writer," I said.

She looked up at me and beamed as all the kids started clapping.

"And you know what else, JoJo? I think I am going to make you our new official writing expert here in Miss Smith's kindergarten classroom," I said.

"Yay, JoJo," Taylor cheered.

"This is something you need to keep working on, and you'll just get better and better," I told her.

She looked up at me. "Like you, Miss Raymond?"

"Like me? What do you mean?" I was confused.

"Like your running?" she said, eyes widening innocently, and I felt happiness spread through my chest.

"Yes, like me. Thanks, JoJo." She really was an awesome kid.

"Okay, class, let's get ready for lunch," Fiona announced.

Several kids raced to their cubbies to grab their lunch boxes and others shuffled around, putting up pencils and papers.

"I'm really going to miss having you in my class

in January, Kells," Fiona said with a big sigh. "But I agree with JoJo. You just keep getting better and better—not only in running, but in your teaching as well."

"Thanks, Fi. Now I just need to figure out how in the world I can finish the coursework—or at least start," I said.

While the kids finished lining up, I went over to my cubby to grab my own lunch box, but my path was blocked when Tricia walked into our room and made a beeline for me. Her hands were behind her back.

"Miss Raymond, you have a delivery," she said in a sing-song voice, as she revealed a basket with beautiful flowers. These are for you." She handed me the mini wooden bourbon barrel. Its wooden vase was full of tall, fresh green stalks topped with beautiful purple flowers, and the basket was tied with a smooth white ribbon on the outside. The lavender fragrance permeated the entire classroom.

"Wow!" Fiona said, taking in the spray of flowers. "I've never seen such a beautiful bouquet of lavender."

"Miss Raymond has a boyfriend," JoJo said in a sing-song manner, and I felt my cheeks flush.

"*Oooh*," the kids chorused. "K-i-s-s-i-n-g."

I forgot where I was for a moment. I couldn't remember the last time I'd received flowers. I gently touched one of the buds, stunned.

"Read the card," Fiona whispered, pulling it out of the vase and handing it to me.

I read it silently.

"What? You cannot just read it to yourself." Fiona said, "I have to hear what it says."

"'Are your legs tired?'" I read aloud, "'because

you've been running through my mind all day. If that cheesy line doesn't make you literally run—call or text me if you'd like to meet again -Erik.' Oh, and below his name is his cell phone number."

"Kells, you have to call or text him right away," Fiona squealed, reading over my shoulder.

"Yes," the kids said, like a chorus of little Cupids.

"What do I say?" My cheeks immediately burned.

"I can tell you something to write," JoJo stepped forward.

"She's the class expert on writing. Remember, Miss Raymond?" Taylor said.

I had twenty-five sets of ears all listening and watching my reaction. I bit my lip and finally said, "Okay, Cyrano, give me my lines." I took out my phone.

JoJo thought for a few seconds, and then dictated, "Some roses are red. Some flowers are purple. I want to see you, too—you flurple."

I typed her words into a new text, and then added a postscript: "JoJo from school wrote this for me. I look forward to hearing from you. The flowers are gorgeous."

"Friday at seven," came the immediate reply from Erik.

"*Oooo!*" the class cheered. "Miss Raymond has a boyfriend."

I loved the thought.

~ Twenty-Four ~

"If you don't feel like running, go anyway. Go on a walk, do something—keep persevering."
-Amy, runner for fifteen years

"Hellloooo, anyone home?" I yelled into the house. Nobody answered. "Amelia?" Still silence. *She must be at school still.*

I slugged up the stairs and changed my clothes. I slowly pulled on my workout clothes. I glanced at my bed and yearned for a nap. As I walked back down the stairs and toward the garage door, I caught a glimpse of my favorite recliner.

Just a few minutes, I told myself, and sank into the chair lifting the footrest up high for maximum comfort and relaxation.

I stared at my sneakers, trying to think of a good excuse to kick them off and stay in this cloud of comfort, daydreaming about Erik. I stretched my neck a tad and glanced out the window, hoping for a sudden shower. Just the motion of moving my head made me even more tired. *Come on, Kentucky, where are your good ol' clouds?*

Maybe a huge thundercloud had moved in since I came home from work, and I would have to stay inside for days, curled up with unsweetened hot chocolate and a good book. I kicked my sneakers off in anticipation.

Of course, it would need to clear up by Friday night at seven o'clock. That evening would be completely clear with millions of stars twinkling in

173

the sky. It would be a little cooler, and I would mention the chill in the air. Erik would take off his jacket and drape it around my shoulders, enveloping me in his clean, crispy, woodsy scent.

But tonight, I needed a break. I peeked out the window again. The sky was perfectly clear—blue skies, without a cloud in sight.

I pulled on my sneakers and tied the laces in double knots. If I had learned anything while running so far, I had learned you needed to tie double knots, otherwise you could trip or have to keep stopping.

That's it. I smiled as I untied my sneakers and tied each shoe in a single knot, thinking that at least this would give me some breaks while running.

I wriggled my toes around inside my shoe. Something felt strange. I yanked off my right sneaker and discovered a small hole in my sock near my pinky toe. I grabbed the sock—and *oops*—it ripped a little bit more. *Perfect.*

I texted Georgia:

> *Hole in socks. Can't run.*
> *Don't want blisters.*

I closed my eyes and relaxed deeper into the recliner. I needed a break. Amelia's problems stressed me out, and I still hadn't done anything about signing up for classes at UK. I was exhausted just thinking about it all.

My cell phone buzzed.

Fiona texted back:

> *Super lame excuse. Meet at*
> *Jesse's Run Shop in 20 min.*
> *We'll get you socks, and Georgia*
> *some new sneakers. Then we'll*
> *run in Lexington at the arboretum.*

What? I pushed the footrest down and sat up.

Twenty minutes? Can't do it. But actually, I could.

Why did I ask Fiona to run with me? She's crazy determined and disciplined. No fairy tale character could describe her. Fiona was pure super-hero.

~ * ~

When I walked into Jesse's Run Shop, the girls were already there. Georgia relaxed in a chair while a young woman measured her foot.

Fiona stood next to her, hair pulled back, decked out in a chic running ensemble that made her look like Georgia's personal trainer. I smiled. That would be her superhero name—Captain Personal Trainer.

"Nice try," Fiona said the moment she spotted me. "I do declare," she said, imitating me. "'I couldn't possibly run today.'"

I crossed my arms and made a face. "I worked all day. I'm tired. Besides, I really do need new socks."

"And I need new shoes," Georgia said, waving her pointed toe in the air. The worker measured her Fit on the metal plate. "What do you think? Should I get two pairs? One pink and one flurple?" Georgia burst out laughing.

"Eight and a half," the worker said. "Please place your other foot here." She moved the metal plate, and Georgia stepped on it.

I rolled my eyes. "Very funny, Georgia. I see you and Fi have been exchanging stories about me."

"I'm serious about getting a couple of pairs. You know, maybe to alternate support or something?" Georgia bounded over to the wall of sneakers and pointed at one shoe. "I love this style." She moved slightly and pointed at another. "Oh, these are cute. I love this color."

"You should get sneakers that are good for what

175

you *need*," the young girl interjected. "Let's look at your stride now that I've measured your foot. Then we'll make sure you have the perfect sneaker for what you need."

"Kells, socks are over here." Fiona grabbed my arm and pulled me to a wall of socks. "You needed socks, right?"

I pulled up my running pants and glanced at my ankles.

"Kells. Your socks are supposed to match, or are you going for the Pippi-Longstocking look like JoJo? I guess you really did need socks."

"I told you I did."

"Come on ladies, let's get this show on the road. We're still running today, so get your goods and let's get going."

~ * ~

Georgia and I left our cars in the parking lot at Jesse's Run Shop and jumped into Fiona's BMW™.

The inside smelled like lemons and was immaculate. Not a crumb in sight, unlike my truck, which usually had fast-food wrappers and empty diet peach tea bottles everywhere.

"You know, Fiona," Georgia said, "we could always stop and get ice cream instead of run—"

"Enough excuses already, you two," Fiona said. "We're running today. Besides, you have to try out your new sneakers." She looked at Georgia first and then me. "And socks."

We pulled into the arboretum and parked. It looked like the setting from a fairytale, with tree-lined paths branching out every which way, dotted with people jogging and walking dogs. I suddenly felt motivated to run. Fiona was right, we needed a change of pace.

"How do we know how long the paths are?" I asked, as we stretched.

"I'm not sure exactly how long they are, but we can watch the time." Fiona glanced at her watch. "Let's go."

Our running plan was called "Couch to 5K," and I had taken that literally today. It was week six, but I had to admit the running app was helping. Despite having been on the couch (well, recliner) just before our workout, I didn't feel too horrible when we broke into a brisk walk.

I oversaw our workout app today. I pulled out my phone and started week six, day two. Our routine would be walk for five minutes to warm-up, jog for ten minutes, and walk for three minutes. This was going to be a tough day.

We began our brisk walk and then broke into a run. It seemed both Georgia and I were running along with less effort than normal. We were keeping up with Fiona, running side-by-side.

I opened my mouth and broke out into song, "Set your soles on fi—." I tripped on my shoelace, and Georgia caught me before I could fall on my face.

I stopped and bent down. Out of the corner of my eye, I saw Georgia and Fiona exchange looks. "Hey, I know that look. What are you...?" And before I could finish, they raced off.

"Set those soles on fire and catch up, girlfriend," Georgia said. I yanked the shoelaces and fiddled with the stupid knot, silently chastising my past couch-chair self.

~ Twenty-Five ~

"After an awesome training run, I feel rejuvenated, and I know the rest of my day will go better."
-Meredith, runner for one year

On Friday, I raced around the house trying to find my keys, but I didn't dare text Fiona I'd be late because I couldn't find my keys. I knew she would think I was making more excuses not to run or something. I stopped and tried to remember the last place I had them.

My phone buzzed, and I opened a group message from Georgia to Fiona and me:
> *Sorry. Can't run.*
> *Gracie is sick.*
> *C U Mon.*

I quickly texted back:
> *Hope she feels better soon.*
> *Luv that grl!*

Fiona texted back almost simultaneously:
> *Sorry, Georgia. C U Mon.*

And then I received a text from Fiona:
> *U r on ur own. Can't make it today <3*
> *Shruti needs help.*

I shot back to Fiona:
> *Nooooo!*

Fiona responded:
> *Sorry. I need to help Shruti.*

My heart sank, and I pulled out the kitchen chairs to sit down, and there, shining back up at me were my keys. It was definitely a sign. I had to run.

Resigned, I pulled on my new socks and laced up my sneakers while I tried to hum my Drake Douglas tune to pump myself up. It cheered me up a tad. *Music*, I thought, *that's what I need*. I remembered buying an armband for Amelia. She claimed she needed it for gym class or something. I never saw her wear it. *Hmmm*. I headed up to her room. "It has to be in here someplace," I muttered to myself.

I looked around her room. Clothes were all over the floor, and papers were scattered all over her bed.

At first glance, I thought they were college applications. I smiled, thankful that maybe she was finally taking the whole college thing seriously. I leaned over to take a little look to see where she was applying.

There was someone's handwriting on a sticky note on one of the papers. It wasn't Amelia's handwriting. She never wrote that neatly.

> *I thought you might be*
> *interested...*
> *Blessings,*
> *M.*

M? Monica? What in the world? I peeled off the note and examined the paper underneath.

United Women's Chorus was printed across the top. The description was as follows:

> *An amazing gap-year program*
> *for high school graduates interested*
> *in singing and traveling abroad.*
> *Come and experience the world*
> *through song. Discover new places,*
> *new friends, and new music.*
> *Applications due by December 10.*
> *Semi-finalist auditions*

will be held in mid-December.
Finalists will be selected by January 1.
$500.00 deposit due by January 10.

My heart pounded. *Why did Monica send this to Amelia?* Surely it was from Monica since I couldn't think of anyone else Amelia knew who had a name that started with "M". This must be her way of stopping Amelia from going to college. I threw the paper down on the bed and grabbed another.

"'Eton Chorus will be the best year of your life,'" I read. "What? Eaton Chorus?"

I frantically sifted through the remaining papers. None of them were for college. There were four more applications to gap programs that involved music. Tears flooded my eyes. I dropped the stack of papers and wiped my face with the back of my hand.

I decided right after Jake left that I wouldn't cry for things that were out of my control. *But* did *I have control over this? What right did Monica have to send these to my daughter?*

I took several of the papers, making sure to get the sticky note, too. I felt hot, hotter than I did while running in ninety-degree heat. These needed to go in the trash. My daughter's future was too important. I didn't know if I was more hurt that Monica sent these and Amelia didn't tell me, or that Amelia was applying to gap-year programs and not colleges. She had lied to me by omission.

For a moment, I paused. Did *she tell me she was going to apply for a gap program?* Even after all our arguments, I didn't think she was truly considering not going to college.

A picture of Oxford on the cover of one of the

gap-year programs caught my attention. I flopped onto her bed, crushing multiple papers underneath me, and read the brochure from cover-to-cover.

Amelia could travel to England and sing?

I glanced back at the papers on her bed. They were in shambles. It was a mess.

I looked over at her nightstand drawer. Her armband was right there. Next to it lay her journal. I froze. *Should I?*

They say, 'curiosity killed the cat.' I smiled and shrugged. *Thank goodness I'm not a cat.* I grabbed her journal and opened it to the most recent entry.

Pros:
I love to sing
I could take time to figure out what I want to do for my career
I have always wanted to travel
It is paid for. No debt

Cons:
Mom doesn't want me to go
I will be a year behind in college,
I probably couldn't get in anyway. It's a stupid dream.
Stupid idea.
I can't sing.

I dropped the journal. *Amelia is a dreamer, just like me.* I felt horrible and elated. Confused. Guilt-stricken. I needed to clear my head. I needed to *run*.

~ * ~

It seemed strange to run alone. The sidewalk stretched out before me like a never-ending path. Without my friends to occupy my attention, I was stuck with my own thoughts racing in my head.

I put in my headphones and put my playlist on shuffle, and then slipped my phone into Amelia's armband and strapped it to my arm.

Drake Douglas's song was the first to come on. I took a deep breath and started to jog.

I pictured myself in a deep green floor-length dress, dancing at a Christmas ball with Erik. *Yes, I will imagine myself dancing with Erik*, I thought. *That will take my mind off everything.*

I conjured up poinsettias decorating a ballroom with Christmas music playing in the background. The party guests were in great spirits, and Erik and I danced in the center of them. He twirled me around the dance floor. When the song ended, we stopped dancing and clapped. I glanced around and noticed a stage. Amelia was standing center front before the microphone. She smiled and dropped into an elegant curtsy. Monica was on stage with her, waving to the audience. Amelia stopped smiling when she saw me and walked off the stage.

The song on my cell phone changed, snapping me out of the imagined scenario. *Why does Monica even get to ruin my daydreams?* I shook my head and tried to concentrate on the music in my ears. The *real* music. I didn't need to imagine Erik, or dancing, or Amelia singing to feel better. I realized I felt better just from the run.

Before I knew it, I was jogging at a brisk pace. The song reverberated through my mind. *Run to your dreams. Run to your dreams.* Then the bridge of the song:

"Without a car, she didn't think she could make it farther than city limits,

But she squared her shoulders, and thought of how her mamma told her

To keep the faith, fight the fight, and run the race."

I yanked out my headphones and ran until I didn't even notice the sidewalk anymore—even the trees along the path were a green and brown blur. The lyrics morphed into my thoughts, and I could feel all my negative energy falling away. Finally, I slowed to a walk and checked my timer. While wiping hard-earned sweat from my brow, I did a double take on my app.

I had run an entire 5K route without walking, without stopping, and without feeling out of breath or too weak. My head felt light, and not from exhaustion—this time, I felt only pride and pure joy.

~ Twenty-Six ~

"One time when I was in the locker room, after working out, a butt-naked lady said to me, 'I love your shoes.' I felt like I should compliment her, because I always try to compliment people back, but she was totally nude! What are you supposed to compliment? She did have a really good body—she was probably in her sixties, and she was in very good shape, but I thought it would be weird to comment on that. So, I just said, 'Thank you!'"
—Julia, runner for nine years

Amelia was home when I returned from my run.

"Hi," she said breezily, then took in my appearance. "Mom, you look like a red Christmas ball."

"Good to see you, too," I said, still bursting with pride from my run. Being compared to a red, round ball couldn't ruin my mood, but a sudden jolt of remembrance could. *Had she found the application papers yet? Did she know I went through her room? Oh dear Lord, I do need help.*

"Where have you been?" Amelia asked.

I moved toward her to give her a huge, sweaty hug. "Out and a-boot," I joked.

"Gross, Mom. You're all sweaty." She pushed me away.

"I am?" I said, feigning ignorance. I continued to rush toward her, arms outstretched for a hug, and she leaped out of her chair and raced around the kitchen table.

"You're crazy."

"I am, and guess what, you've got fifty percent of my genes." I laughed and moved toward her once again. Amelia screamed, and then broke into a laugh that matched mine.

"So, Mom, I was wondering," she said, once she was sure I wasn't going to drip sweat all over her, "could you take me shopping tonight to get new shoes for the Holiday Spectacular? I need them for practice."

Whew. She hasn't been to her room yet.

"I thought you were quitting," I said carefully.

"Why would I quit? I love singing. You know that."

"*Mmmmhmmm*, I'm actually glad to hear that. But as much as I love shopping with you...I kind of have a date tonight." I could feel my cheeks flush. Thank goodness my face was already red from running.

"You have a date? What?" Amelia said, clapping her hands together.

"It's nothing serious, just a dinner date." I bit my lip to stop myself from breaking into a Cheshire Cat smile.

"Who are you going out with? Why didn't I know about this?"

"You haven't really wanted to talk with me much lately," I said softly. I didn't want to guilt-trip her, but it was true.

"I know, Momma," Amelia said, her eyes tearing. "I'm sorry. It's just that you want me to go to college, and I want to sing. I've been thinking about..." She trailed off, probably expecting me to make some comment about how I didn't want to get into it.

"A gap year singing. I know," I said. "I saw the brochures on your bed." I never was good at keeping secrets.

Amelia's countenance shifted instantly. "You went into my room?"

I nodded my head.

"When I wasn't home?"

I nodded again.

"I can't believe you were snooping in my room." She stood up and angrily pushed her chair away from the table.

"I wasn't snooping, Amelia. I went in to get your armband for my run, and I saw those brochures. It was hard to miss. They were all over your bed spread out for all the word to see. I was upset at first—"

"How could you look at the stuff in my room?"

"Amelia, just listen—after I looked them over, I went for my run," I said. "While I was running, I was listening to Drake's song, *Running to Your Dreams*, and I thought, *Amelia needs to run to her dreams, too. She's right. She has been telling me this, and I haven't been listening.*" I reached over and touched her arm. "Honey, if you don't want to go to college yet, then you know what, I'll support whatever you decide."

"Wait, what?" Her eyes widened in disbelief.

"Amelia, if you want to sign up for a gap year program—or move to Nashville, whatever you want to do this next year—I'll support you," I said. "I hope you'll consider going to college after the gap year, but if you want to sing first, you need to go for it."

"Are you serious?" She stood up from the chair, dropped her arms by her side, and stared at me in disbelief. "Seriously?" She held her breath.

My words surprised me too, but as I spoke them I

knew they were the right ones. For once. "Amelia, you are so talented. If singing is your passion, and that's what you'd like to do, then I think you should go for it. Other people do it—why not you?"

"Oh, Momma." She ran over and pulled me into a bear hug, despite my sweat. Tears swelled up in my eyes, and I blinked them away, along with thoughts of Amelia leaving. I really was going to miss her.

"You know, that program in Oxford looked pretty amazing," I said, dabbing at my eyes. "As long as I could come and visit while you're there."

"Yes. Yes. Yes." Amelia broke away from the hug. "Wait a minute—I almost forgot, you have a hot date tonight. I want all the details while I pick out your outfit. Can I pick out your outfit?"

I nodded. "I didn't say 'hot' but I guess--"

"Momma," she said, grabbed my arm, and pulled me up the stairs. "You're going to look so amazing. Just leave it all to me."

I followed her upstairs, feeling happier than a kid on Christmas morning.

Amelia rifled through my closet while I jumped in the shower.

"What if he walks in the house? The kitchen is a mess," I yelled from the bathroom.

"Momma, he's not the cleaning police," Amelia said, and I could practically see her rolling her eyes. "You can meet him at the door."

"What time is it?" I said, rinsing off my lavender-scented body wash.

"Six forty-five."

"Heavens to Betsy, I'm not going to be ready," I said, rinsing faster. "He'll be here in fifteen minutes. He'll imagine I'm a sloth."

187

"Momma. You're almost there. You can do this—we can do this. I'm just about r-e-a-d-y." She slowly spelled out the word. I couldn't see her, but I knew she was looking through my closet.

I threw open the shower curtain. "What am I wearing? Can you hand it to me through the door?"

"Got it. This is perfect," she said, pushing an outfit into my outstretched hand.

She picked out a comfortable yet stylish outfit, blending her fashion skills with my practicality: I pulled on a navy skirt and white lace top, and accessorized with my favorite pearl earrings.

I hoped he'd show up at least a few minutes late. Punctuality was seriously overrated when it came to dates.

I couldn't believe I was going out, and I hadn't had enough time to get ready properly. I flipped on my blow dryer with one hand and dumped a few makeup products on my vanity with the other. My face was still red as a Christmas bulb. I swiped on mascara. The doorbell rang and I jumped, sending a streak of black across my cheek with the wand.

"Amelia, can you get that?" I said, dabbing frantically at my cheek.

"You've got this," she said cheerfully.

I finished with the makeup, hoping I had somewhat masked my red cheeks.

I tried to throw my sweater over my shoulders while I raced down the stairs, but it landed on top of my head at the very moment I swung open the door.

"Hi," I said through the light purple arm of my sweater.

Erik grabbed my sweater arm and shook it. "Hello," he said. "Great to see you again, Kelly Jo."

I pulled the sweater off my head. My cheeks

burned.

Amelia stood behind Erik and mouthed, *He's so hot*. I nodded my head slightly, and she raised her eyebrows up and down.

"You need a little help with that *flurple* sweater?" Erik grinned. He wore a crisp blue button down with the sleeves rolled up and looked completely put together and oh so fine.

"I need more than a little help," I laughed, and felt my cheeks burn even hotter. "Wait. That came out wrong."

Erik untangled the sweater from my head and tied it gently around my shoulders. He was so close to me that I could smell his cologne. I was light-headed from his wonderful light, wooded scent. Crisp. Clean.

"I knew exactly what you meant," he winked, and I melted inside.

~ Twenty-Seven~

"One time, during a run with my friend from my neighborhood, I got chased by a skunk at dusk, and we ran to get away from it onto the golf course—the sprinklers came on just as we did!"
-Joni, runner for five years

The restaurant Erik chose was trendy and modern inside. There were huge fish tanks with tropical fish swimming lazily around coral reefs. The hostess sat us at a booth with a high, sleek glass table with a miniature evergreen centerpiece covered in tiny fish ornaments.

"I've never been here before," I said, sliding into the booth. "This building is beautiful."

It was two stories, and we were on the upper floor, a balcony surrounding the interior of the building, giving us a view of the tables below.

"You flatter me," Erik said, picking up a menu.

"What?" I asked, taking a menu. I skipped the page listing sushi—no way I was going to eat fish with all of them swimming in tanks around me.

"It's my design," he said, and for once it was his turn to blush. "I guess I was showing off by bringing you here, but the owner is a friend and he gave me creative license. I'm sort of proud of the result."

"You should be," I said, in awe, looking around at the design of the actually building. "I love the beams, the way they open up the ceiling. It's beautiful."

"Do you think so?" He leaned forward.

"Definitely."

We ordered drinks and I sat back, still admiring the building.

"I always knew you'd be successful, even back in high school. You always drew the most beautiful designs in your sketchbook. I remember it, all of us in youth group were obsessed with you—I mean, with your drawings." My face grew hot, and I grabbed my drink, stirring it around and around with the skinny little straw.

"Are you kidding me? *You* were the one everyone knew would be successful," Erik said, leaning forward.

"Me?" I asked. "Nobody would say that."

"Always the first to raise your hand, the first to know the answer—you were so fearless. I always admired that."

I knit my brows together. I never thought of myself as fearless, though I'd always wanted to be. *Had* I been? *Why didn't I think I was strong or fearless now?*

The waitress placed my cocktail on the table, not aware her sleeve caught on the glass's edge. I watched as the drink spilled, sticky pink liquid soaking into my white blouse. *This can't be happening.*

The waitress clapped her hand over her mouth, her eyes welling with tears. "Oh no. I'm so sorry. It's my first day, and I knew something like this was going to happen, especially when the architect—"

"Don't worry about it." I dabbed at the damp blotch with a napkin. "Really, it could happen to anyone. It's happened to me." I winked at Erik.

"I'll get more napkins," she said, darting off.

"I guess every time we meet, one of us gets

wet." I laughed, and then covered my mouth. "That definitely came out wrong. I'm going to go dry off in the bathroom. I mean...you know what I mean."

If being fearless meant that I said whatever popped into my mind, I was fearless.

In the bathroom, I pumped the soap into my hand and hoped it would do the trick. I scrubbed and scrubbed. I stood on my tippy toes to look up in the mirror. My whole side of my blouse was soaking wet. I crouched down under the automatic hand dryer and dried the blouse the best I could. Sighing, I checked my reflection in the mirror once again. *Doesn't look too bad.* I tucked my blouse back into my skirt and headed out of the bathroom.

A flash of dark hair caught my eye, and my blood suddenly chilled in my veins. There, at a table across the restaurant, was Monica with her perfect dark hair shining in the light of the open restaurant. My restaurant. She was with her husband, Michael. He was in a white crisp shirt and Kentucky blue tie. I could see his blue eyes sparkle as he talked. Monica threw her head back and laughed. I stood still feeling like my feet were stuck in cement. I imagined the walls of the restaurant imploding and all that was left was me standing with a soaking wet blouse and Monica sitting with her husband and the other friends, still sitting, drinking, eating at the table, and all laughing at me. *Nooooo. Not tonight.* I couldn't move. I blinked. I blinked again.

Sitting across from Monica and Michael was Jake, Amelia's father and my ex-boyfriend from college. Jake had his arm draped around the shoulders of a skinny redhead, and they were both laughing at something. Smiling smugly, sensing my presence and knowing this would get under my skin, Monica sipped primly from a wine glass.

I wanted to punch something. Preferably Monica's perfectly pink-lipstick pout. I didn't advocate violence, but in this case, maybe it would resolve the anger that rushed through my veins.

Was my imagination in high gear tonight? Monica, my once best-confidante, my best friend, on a double date with my old ex? Had they been friends all these years? It's not like I expected her to choose sides after the breakup—*wait, what?* Of *course*, I expected her to choose sides. And she should have chosen *mine*. She should have chosen to be by my side eighteen years ago, instead of leaving me high and dry.

I pulled out my phone and snapped a picture of the four of them, unable to help myself. For some reason I wanted proof that what I had seen was real and not some crazy daydream...well, nightmare. *What is her problem? Why does she constantly hurt me like this?*

It wasn't the leggy redhead that bothered me—it was Monica's betrayal. I sent the picture to Fiona, Georgia, and Shruti. My phone immediately buzzed.

I returned to Erik, but I couldn't shake the deep anger that was settling in the pit of my stomach.

"Almost as good as new," I said as I slipped into my seat, gesturing to my shirt. My phone buzzed again.

"You look great, Kelly Jo," he said with a smile.

My phone buzzed another time.

"This truly is a beautiful restaurant," I said, trying to get back into our stride prior to my Monica spotting. "Even the bathroom was amazing."

My phone buzzed again, vibrating the entire table. I quickly glanced down at it. Georgia had sent a long response, which I tried to read without being rude and touching the screen.

Erik raised his eyebrows. "Do you need to answer that?" he asked.

I shook my head. "No, it's fine."

He kept staring at my phone, and it buzzed again. It was Fiona. I tossed it into my purse.

"Where were we?" I said, my heart plummeting when I saw Erik's frown. I pulled my sweater up and around my arms to try and shake the chill I felt in the room.

"We were reminiscing, I think," he said, and I felt a twinge of unease. His mood had clearly shifted. Ugh. Monica had ruined my first real date out with Erik.

I slung my purse under the table. My heart pounding in my chest.

"Is everything okay?" he asked sitting straighter in his seat.

"Oh, yes. It's fine. I'm fine," I lied grabbing my water glass and drinking the entire glass in one gulp. Erik covered his mouth with his hands. *Was he smiling? Was he suppressing his anger?* For a split second I imagined him storming out and leaving me alone at the table. The noise would attract such a commotion that everyone at Monica's table would look over and see me, still damp from the drink, sitting by myself in utter humiliation.

"Do you remember when we did that ropes course senior year, and we went on that crazy zip line?" I blurted, trying to swallow my panic and will away the horrible image I had conjured. Surely it was all in my head.

To my relief, Erik broke into a wide grin and laughed.

"You screamed so loudly I thought my eardrums were going to shatter."

"Hey, I wasn't the only one screaming."

"It was super high up." He laughed again.

Relief washed over me. *We're back in the groove.*

We ordered, talked, and reminisced. It still seemed a bit strained, because Erik paused and glanced at my purse every time my phone buzzed. I wished I wouldn't have texted that stupid picture.

The meal was delicious. I took a final bite and stared at Erik. *How on earth had I managed to score a date with such an amazing guy?* I dabbed at my mouth with my napkin and placed it back on my lap. My sweater shifted, and I tossed it over my chair. Erik's attention was all the warmth I needed.

~ * ~

Soft country music played over the radio as Erik drove me back to my house. Suddenly, I heard the familiar strains of my favorite song.

"She was from a small town," Drake Douglas sang.

"I love this song," I said excitedly and turned up the volume. "Are you a Drake Douglas fan?"

"Can't say I've listened to him much, but I like this song."

I belted along with the radio. "Set your soles on fire, blaze ahead at full speed..."

Erik laughed, his eyes crinkling at the corners and turning me into a blob of gelatin. "Is this your anthem, Kelly Jo Raymond?"

"Kind of."

He pulled up to a red stoplight. "I've had a great time. Would you want to come over to my house for S'mores?"

"Really?" I blinked. "S'mores?"

"S'mores and conversation," he said, holding my gaze. I gulped. *Wow, his eyes are beautiful.*

"I would love some more," I whispered.

He drove us to his house, a small ranch with a rustic wooden door, not far from my neighborhood. He led me to the back porch, where there was a small fire pit and several Adirondack chairs.

"I'll split some wood," he said, rolling up his sleeves. "Want to grab the chocolate and marshmallows? They're inside in my pantry, behind the two sliding barn-doors in the kitchen."

I wandered around his kitchen and admired how neat everything was. *Handsome, kind,* and *clean?* I blinked. This man was a dream come true.

I grabbed a bag of marshmallows and a package of milk chocolate bars out of the pantry. I looked at the labels to count the calories and sugar content, but then I stopped.

"Not tonight," I whispered. I turned the package around so I couldn't see how many grams of badness were in the delicious treat. Tonight was a freebie.

I looked out the window and saw Erik building the fire. He chopped wood with an axe, and then placed the wood in a fire pit. A small flame crackled to life. I watched from the window and stared at his muscular forearms, then at his kind face.

"Don't mess this one up, Kelly Jo." I tucked in my blouse, smoothed down my skirt, and then stepped out onto the porch, brandishing the S'mores supplies.

"Ready for some sugar?" I said cheerily, and then felt my cheeks immediately go red. *Why couldn't I say two words to this man without putting my foot in my mouth?*

"I sure am," he said, grinning. "Here, do you need an extra blanket?" He handed me a beautiful flannel quilt. "At least, until the fire gets started."

"This is beautiful."

"My mom made it."

I threw it over my legs.

We roasted marshmallows and chatted cozily. The crickets hummed, and the stars lit up the backyard like sparkling lights. Despite the fact I was usually an indoorsy person, I felt the most relaxed I had been in a while. I took in another deep breath and relished the cool night air.

After what felt like mere minutes, my phone buzzed. I looked down and saw that it was past midnight.

"It's midnight—I probably should be heading home," I said reluctantly.

Erik smiled, leaned in, and my phone buzzed. My stupid, horrible, idiotic phone.

"Sorry," I said.

"Maybe you should look at it. It's been buzzing all night long."

"I'm sure it's fine."

I looked quickly at my screen. The girls were still responding to my group text about Monica at the restaurant. All of that seemed far away now.

I set my phone on "do not disturb" and looked up and leaned in hoping Erik would lean in again, too. Instead, he stood and quickly walked over to the fire and started to spread the wood all around, causing the flame to immediately fade. *Had he seen my phone?* Fiona had sent the picture back to me with a caption,

"What in the world, Kelly Jo? Are you still with Erik? Call me ASAP."

"You're right, it's late. I should take you back."
Dang technology, I cursed silently.

Erik was quiet during the entire drive to my house. When I opened the door in my driveway, he mumbled, "Good night," walked me silently to my door, turned, then sped away.

I stood at my doorway with the door wide open transfixed on the empty street. Everything had been so great, until the picture. *Did he see me? Had I misinterpreted everything? Had I said something wrong?*

No. I am done with ruts and negative thoughts. He's probably just shy, I reassured myself. I refused to let my imagination spoil one of the best nights ever.

~ Twenty-Eight ~

"I remember being in a race one time and watching an older man run in front of me. I was thinking, 'that is such a terrible gate—that must be painful,' but then I realized he was faster than me. Running is humbling in that sense."
-Bethany, runner for thirty-two years

"Kelly Jo how was your hot date Friday night?" Fiona asked. "I waited all weekend. All day today. No calls. No texts. Except that picture. What in the world happened?"

"You know I was testing kiddos all day today at school. I couldn't talk."

"Um, Kells. It has been three days and you are still not talking. What's up? Come on. Let's walk and you talk."

We started our warm-up walk around the cul-de-sac.

"Spill it girlfriend. We need details," Georgia said, picking up the pace in anticipation.

"Hey, this is supposed to be our warm-up time," I protested.

"If you're going to talk about a hot and steamy date, we'll have to pick up our pace," Fiona shot back. "In fact, we may have to add a few miles to our workout today, to ensure we get every last detail."

"There isn't much to tell, other than it was amazing, perfect, horrible, and miserable all at the same time."

"What do you mean?" Fiona asked. "If Erik hurt you, gorgeous construction worker or not, he is going—"

"No," I said. "No, it was Monica. Only Monica. Monica double-dating with Jake. She ruined my dream date." I started pumping my arms and sped ahead of them.

"Hey girl, we're walking, remember?" Georgia said.

"Monica ruins everything," I said.

We rounded the corner, done with our little cul-de-sac and street warm-up, and started toward the main street.

"Let's run," the app chirped.

"Can you talk and run?" Fiona asked. "If not, we can just walk. This is way more important, Kells."

"I can run," I said quickly. "I need to run."

I took off, jogging faster than our normal pace. My quads started to burn, but I didn't care. I kept running.

I took a deep breath and recounted the entire evening. The running only gave me energy to spill it all.

"So why was you-know-who on a double date with Jake?" Fiona asked as she picked up the pace and started running just in front of Georgia. "Has she been friends with him all these years?"

I tried to speak, but I was trying too hard to keep up with her.

"Doesn't she remember what that man did to you?" Fiona continued. "Leaving you all by yourself with a baby? Really. How could someone do that?" She stopped. "How could someone—"

Georgia ran right into Fiona, and I nearly collided with them.

"I know, right?" I bent over, trying to catch my breath in the shade of the huge evergreen tree next to the sidewalk. "I keep trying to let it all go, but then I keep seeing her. And I keep rehashing everything, and I feel like..." Something warm plopped on my shoulder and dripped slowly down my arm. "You've got to be kidding me."

Fiona took one look at me and erupted into laughter. Her chuckling burst beyond her fingers and popped the air like opening a new bag of potato chips. Georgia and I laughed until we had tears rolling down our faces.

"Nothing like getting crapped on by a bird to make light of a situation. You certainly are quite the woman," Georgia said, her face streaming with tears.

"You know what, Kells?" Fiona said, pulling a moist towelette out of her shorts pocket and handing it to me. "I think you need to clean up this mess and let it go."

"Where in the world did that come from?" I asked looking at the little towelette package.

Fiona pulled out another towelette from her pocket, wiped off the rest of the bird poop on me as if I were one of her kindergarteners, and exclaimed, "We're done with CRAP, Kelly Jo Raymond." My eyes bulged. "This is it," Fiona continued. "I know you won't say it, but I'm gonna say it for you. I am so done with Monica Shmonica. The next time I see her, I'm going to give her a piece of my mind."

"Really, Fi? Shmonica? That's all you've got?" Georgia said, putting a hand on one hip. "I could think of a lot more names to call that woman."

"It's the best I've got... After all, I work with kindergarteners," Fiona said with a shrug.

I grinned. Kindergarten insults were fine by me.

"I do need to stop letting her get under my skin." I took a deep breath. "I need to move on. Besides, I have other things to worry about. Like, why did Erik act so weird after my phone buzzed during our date? Does he have something against technology?"

"I'm sure it's fine," Fiona said, pulling me to my feet.

"It's probably just your imagination," Georgia said.

We took off running once more, rounded the next corner, and jogged the rest of the way to the parking lot.

"Sorry ladies, I've got an appointment. I've gotta go," Fiona said. "We'll finish the talk later. And don't forget to stretch."

"Thanks for the pep talk."

"Anytime," she said, and jogged straight to her car, faster than our workout pace. That woman was impressive.

"I can't stretch today, Kells," Georgia said, tapping her rhinestone-encrusted wristwatch. "I gotta pick up Gracie from gymnastics."

I waved at Georgia and headed to my truck. While I walked, I noticed a silver F-150™ coming up the hill in the distance. It had to be Erik's truck.

I raced over to get a closer look. It *was* his truck. At least I thought it was his truck.

Without hesitation, I threw my thumb in the air like a crazy hitchhiker and waved with my other hand.

Erik glanced my way. Our eyes locked. He lifted his fingers off the steering wheel and gave a slight wave, but then gripped the wheel and looked away.

No smile. No honk. He just drove on by, leaving me standing by the side of the road with my thumb in the air feeling dumb as a post.

~ Twenty-Nine ~

"After a training run I feel better, and I feel like I have accomplished something."
-*Amy, runner for fifteen years*

"I'm absolutely starving." I stood in front of the refrigerator, pressing the top of my head on a chilled gallon of fat free milk.

I was still burning up from my after-school training run. Fiona had decided we would take a new route. Every time our timer told us to run, it was up a hill. When the timer beeped, ready to give us a walking break, we were already on the way down. Every. Stinking. Time. I was exhausted, my legs were killing me, and I was hot and famished.

"How about pizza? Pleeeeease?" Amelia yelled from upstairs. "We could even get the diet kind."

"Yes." I pulled up the number for Pizazz Pizza on my cell, and my mouth began to water. At this point, I was sure I could eat an entire truckload of pizza, so finishing off a "diet" one would be a piece of cake.

Ooh. Don't think about cake, I reminded myself mentally. *One thing at a time*. I punched in the number.

"Pizazz Pizza. Will this be for delivery or carry-out?"

"Delivery. I'll take two small pizzas, please, extra thick crust. One pepperoni, one Hawaiian," I said quickly. I didn't need a diet pizza or a reduced-fat cheese pizza. I needed the real thing, and I needed an entire real thing. Sometimes a person just had to treat herself.

"We should have a TV night," Amelia said, bounding into the room. "Or do you have another hot date?"

"Yes, and no," I said quickly. "And I was thinking the same thing. I'll just take a quick shower before the Pepperoni and Hawaiian pizza comes."

"Pepperoni and Hawaiian, seriously?"

"You know it," I said, grinning at her.

I raced upstairs with newfound energy, excited for the time with my sweet girl.

~ * ~

Amelia and I sat on the couch while *Gilmore Girls* played in the background.

"Will you paint my left hand?" she asked and handed me a bottle of dark green nail polish. "I always mess it up."

"Of course, honey." I rolled the bottle in my palms and took her hand in mine, remembering when they were baby hands. *How had she grown up so fast?* Scratch that. She would *always* be my sweet baby girl.

"How did your date go last Friday?" Amelia asked while I painted strips of green on her nails. "You never told me." She blew on her nails.

"It was good," I said, staring determinedly at the television.

"No details? And why didn't you go out again this Friday night?" Amelia asked, pushing me lightly on the shoulder.

"Don't mess up your nails," I said, laughing. "I thought it was *very* good. I like him." I paused, then added, "We couldn't go out this week because he had to travel out of town to place a bid in Cincinnati for a huge new restaurant."

"That's cool," Amelia said, watching my face intently.

"He said he'd text when he knew his upcoming schedule. He mentioned maybe going to this outdoor concert at some winery. This new country singer is playing and singing, and Erik knows I love country music."

"Wow." Amelia sat up straight. "Sounds like this guy and you are a thing."

"We're not a thing. He's not a thing, Amelia. But you know, he is a gentleman." I leaned back on the couch and sighed. "Those are hard to come by, baby girl, but I'm sure you'll meet a few in college—I mean, in your gap-year, or during your travels. So, tell me, which program are you the most interested in?"

Amelia started to discuss the Oxford program, and how difficult it was to get in, when my cell phone buzzed. I glanced down, hoping it was a text from Erik.

It was Fiona:

> *O.R.M. begins. Also known as*
> *Operation Revenge on Monica.*
> *More on Monday.*

"Moooom? Who is it? Who is texting you?" Amelia asked. "Is it him? That Erik dude?"

"No, it's Fi. She wanted to tell me about this plan she has."

Amelia raised one eyebrow. "A plan for what, Momma? Why are you acting so weird?"

I felt a stab of guilt. "Nothing's weird. Everything's fine."

"Mom," Amelia playfully hit my arm, keeping her fingers outstretched.

"Okay, so I saw Monica at the dinner the other

206

night with your dad, and I took a picture on my phone," I said. "Fiona is mad that Monica ruined my night with Erik, but I'm not so sure Monica ruined my night. I think Erik saw the picture, and he's mad. I think he's mad at me." I slumped against my chair, slowly lowering my head on the back, exhausted with the whole situation. At least Amelia and I were done with the no-talking thing, for now.

"Wait, Dad was at dinner with Monica? She's married," Amelia said, shaking her head. "None of this makes sense."

I lifted my head off the chair. "No, your dad was on a double date with Monica and her husband, Michael."

Amelia shrugged. "What's wrong with that?"

I sat straight up in the chair and leaned forward. "You know what, Amelia? I'm not sure now that you ask." I crossed my legs and arms. "I guess I just thought Monica was my friend, not your Dad's."

"She's your friend? I thought you hated her. At least that's the way you act," Amelia said under her breath, one eyebrow still raised.

I looked into Amelia's eyes. I did act like that. She was right. I was so far from the high road that I wasn't even on a road at all. I was lost in the woods. Lost in the treetops.

I grabbed my phone and texted Fiona.

> *Let's talk l8r. Maybe operation—*
> *kindness.*
> *She did help Amelia*
> *with the gap idea.*

I tossed my phone on the coffee table and decided to not think anymore tonight about Monica, Erik, or running, and simply enjoy my time with Amelia.

"What are you singing at the concert, again? *O Holy Night*?"

"Yes. I'm so excited." Her eyes lit up once more, and I felt my troubles drift away.

~ Thirty ~

"I don't really like to run by myself. So, if it weren't for my neighbor, I wouldn't run. I also found that when I don't have a goal, I'm not nearly as motivated."
–Melissa, runner for fourteen years

Fiona's ponytail swished back and forth during our warm-up walk, as she ranted. "You know, Monica is one of those people if you treat her like you want to be treated, she won't notice."

She moved faster, the pace seeming to match her irritation. "She needs to be put in her place."

I shook my head and sighed. "Fiona, Amelia saw our texts. What are we doing? What am I doing? Am I teaching her that revenge is the way to go?"

"Ladies, I'm just here to tell you that our good Lord oversees this revenge stuff, and we need to keep it that way," Georgia cut in, "so can we finally drop this argument and get to discussions about your hot eligible man, Erik Wellsworth?"

I pulled my phone out of my back pocket and glanced at my messages. Nothing.

"Speaking of that hot eligible man, I haven't heard a word from him since he went on his so called, 'business trip.'"

"Are we really going to let this whole Monica thing go? Are we going to just let her do this to Kelly Jo and do nothing? Are we going to just wait around and let her do something else horrible?" Fiona rambled. "Like, I don't know...buy your house, take your job, and leave you homeless?"

I jammed my cell phone back into my pocket and slowed my pace. "Erik—and nothing," I mumbled, "and Georgia's right. Let's forgive and forget. I'm sick of talking about me and all of my messes. Let's talk about you, Fi, or Georgia. What's Gracie up to?"

"Oh, my stars, you would not believe that girl. She kept me up so late last night with an impromptu winter-themed dance and song party. I need to get this run in before my exhausted legs give out."

We walked around the cul-de-sac and started around the bend. We always walked two cul-de-sacs, and then started our run at the mailbox of a little ranch house with blue shutters.

"I feel like we should all sing or something today," I said, "for Gracie, and...to get in the mood for the concert this Friday."

"I can't believe we get to see Drake Douglas in two nights," Fiona said. "I thought I didn't like country music, until you won those tickets, and I started listening to his music nonstop. He's amazing, and he isn't bad on the eyes, either."

"I agree one hundred percent," I said, trying not to think of another man who wasn't bad on the eyes, either. A man named Erik, who couldn't seem to text me back. A chill creeped up my back. I pumped my arms and pulled my knit hat down over my ears.

We passed a house with a blow-up reindeer in the yard, and a huge sleigh with a Santa balloon inside, waving his inflatable arm back and forth.

I imagined Santa taking one look at me and, instead of waving his arm back and forth, shaking his finger back and forth at me.

"I need to be kind," I said in between breaths. "I

need to be a better person—I've been naughty for the last eighteen years, and it's about time I started being nice."

"I've got a stone in my sneaker," Fiona said, ignoring my epiphany. "Do you mind? I need to get it out. It's been driving me crazy."

She yanked off her sneaker and shook it upside down.

Georgia leaned toward me and whispered, "Her turn now?"

I nodded my head, and we took off sprinting.

"Hey," Fiona yelled after we ran off. "I thought you were going to start being nice."

She caught up easily, and we slipped back into pace together.

"Hold up," Georgia said, "look at the adorable lil' pea coat in that store window. It is adorable with that golden piping and fur lining. Wouldn't that look darling on Gracie?" She veered off toward the store before we could protest. Fiona and I jogged over and stood outside the boutique.

"This is running time, not shopping time, woman," Fiona said.

"Maybe we could find a lil' bench or something. She might be a while," I said. We walked toward the bench, and my attention suddenly fixed on a woman across the street. "Fi," I said, grabbing her arm, "Look."

Monica was across the street in front of the town bank, looking put-together and perfect, as usual.

"She's probably planning to rob the joint," I whispered. "I can see it in her eyes."

"You can see her eyes from here?" Fiona snorted.

I squinted at Monica, trying to read her lips.

"Just look at the way she's talking and waving her hands. What do you think she's saying?"

"Who knows *what* that evil woman's up to," Fiona said. "But she's probably simply going to the bank to get cash."

"Yeah, right." I started to move toward Monica, but Fiona pulled me down.

"What about your whole 'kindness' thing?"

"I can't help it. She makes me crazy." I said leaning into the bench, straining my neck around to keep my eyes on Monica.

Fiona turned her entire body around. "Look, she's pacing. She must be nervous about something."

"Now you're imagining things," I whispered. Monica turned in our direction. "Don't let her see us. Squat down." I grabbed Fiona's gloved hand and pulled her around and then behind some evergreen shrubs.

"This is crazy," Fiona breathed as we squatted behind the bushes, keeping her eyes on Monica across the street.

Monica walked over to the bench in front of the bank and sat down, talking animatedly on her phone.

I cupped my hands behind my ears to hear her, and Fiona echoed my motion.

"Yes. Thank you so much," Monica said. "I know that you won't be disappointed, William. Amelia is a beautiful, young girl. Her family could really use the money, too."

"What?" I stood. Fiona instantly grabbed me and pulled me back down behind the bushes.

I bit my cheeks while I leaned around the bush a bit more. Back and forth.

"I can't believe this. She's talking about Amelia. My Amelia. You heard her, right?"

Fiona nodded. "She did all right."

We both peered back to the front of the bank.

Monica placed her phone in her purse, stood, and strode away. I stayed crouched behind the bushes, heart pounding.

"We shouldn't jump to conclusions," Fiona said, "there are a lot of Amelias in the world."

"We both know she was talking about *my* Amelia." I brushed dirt from my hands and stood. "Fi, this is it. Operation Kindness is over, and Operation Revenge begins today."

~ Thirty-One ~

*"I love the running community, the atmosphere,
and how it's super encouraging."
-Cassidy, runner for three years*

I walked into the theater at five-thirty for
Amelia's eight o'clock concert dress rehearsal.
Already, several parents were there ahead of me.
They milled around, carrying tinsel, garlands, and
Christmas-tree-shaped balloons.

"Can you fill these with helium?" One of the
moms shoved a tank and a bag of balloons into my
hands. "We're so far behind. So much needs to be
done."

Amelia ran up to me. "Hi, Momma. Love those
balloons. You're awesome to help. Gotta go." And
she bounded off.

I set down the helium tank and called after her,
"break a leg, sweetie. I'm so proud of you." But she
was already out of earshot.

I sighed. Teenagers were impossible. Had I been
that difficult?

I blew up several balloons and handed them off
to another parent, who transported them into the
auditorium.

While I handed off another balloon bouquet, I
imagined myself floating next to Erik Wellsworth. I
would hold a bundle of balloons in one hand, and he
would hold my other. We would saunter along, Eiffel
Tower in the background.

"Um, Miss Raymond? Miss Raymond, may I have those balloons?"

A voice made my imaginary French daydream disappear, and I looked up to see a student waiting in front of me, hands outstretched.

"Oh, sorry Amy. I was—I mean, here." I shoved the bundle of green balloons into her hand.

After an hour inflating balloons, I made my way into the auditorium with the rest of the parents. I couldn't help but feel a pang of guilt when I looked around at the decorations. *Lord, am I doing the right thing going to my race and missing her concert?* This was huge. I wondered if there would be balloons at the race tomorrow. Surely if I didn't go, Fiona and Georgia would forgive me. They could take pictures, and I could live vicariously through them.

There were colored lights throughout the auditorium, garland and tinsel along the edge of the stage. White snowflakes glittered from the ceiling. The Christmas tree balloons were bunched on either side of the stage, making everything look festive.

The auditorium looked strangely big without a full audience—there were several parents and family members scattered here and there, but I knew that on Friday the auditorium would be packed. It was a sold-out show.

I made my way toward a front row seat but stopped short when I saw Monica sitting on that side of the auditorium. *Seriously?* I turned on my heel and walked to the opposite side of the auditorium. Tonight needed to be a good night without Monica's mean girl energy.

The lights dimmed, and I scrambled into my seat and turned my cell phone to silent mode. No distractions. I closed my eyes briefly, tried to suppress the horrible guilt I felt about still wanting to run with Drake. I opened my eyes and took in a deep breath. I was going to enjoy this moment. Every second.

The a cappella group took the stage. A hush fell over the little audience.

I felt almost starstruck while I watched Amelia blow on her pitch pipe. I relaxed in my seat. She was such a leader. I knew she would be successful in her gap year and beyond, whether she went to college or not. I had worked my way through school and never had much time for fun things like a cappella groups, but life was going to be different for her. It would be different for her because I had worked hard to make sure it was. And so had she. I felt a beam of pride as I leaned forward and rested my arms on the seat in front of me. I focused on Amelia.

~ * ~

The group began their last number with a harmony-filled rendition of *O Holy Night*. It sounded like angels singing. Amelia stepped to the microphone and the choir continued singing quietly in the background. She held up her head and opened her mouth. She wriggled her nose. She twitched.

"*Achoo!*" The microphone screeched. Amelia jumped backwards.

It was the loudest sneeze I've ever heard coming out of that sweet baby girl of mine. Amelia stood like a deer in the headlights on center stage.

The choir froze. The ladies putting up the remaining decorations stopped working. The entire audience was silent. I could hear someone in the audience sniff.

"Sing baby, sing—fall on your knees," I whispered. Still nothing. I moved to the edge of my seat.

"Fall on your knees," I whispered a little louder.

Amelia cleared her throat, stepped back up to the microphone, and without anyone else making a noise, sang, "Faaaaall on your kneeeees, oh heeeeear the angel vooooicees, oh niiiiight divine..." She sounded like Gabriel echoing through the auditorium, and my heart nearly burst with pride. Sure, it was one line, but what a line. And she nailed it.

Suddenly, little paper snowflakes sprinkled onto the stage. Even though I could see the student precariously perched above the stage, dropping them from a big plastic bag, it was still completely magical.

I stood up, clapping like a madwoman, and before I knew it, all of the other parents were doing the same. "Bravo!" I stuck my fingers in my lips and whistled. Amelia looked directly at me and beamed as she stepped forward and took a small bow. She was usually embarrassed when I made a lot of noise, but tonight she didn't seem to mind. She shot me a quick smile. The rest of the group joined her, grabbed hands, and they all bowed. The curtain dropped.

Laughing and talking immediately permeated through the thick curtain and I heard the kids all running into the hallway next to the stage. I leaned down and gathered my belongings and then quickly and politely pushed my way through the other parents into the lobby. I held a bouquet of red roses for Amelia, smelling their sweetness, thinking that maybe everything in life would be sweeter now. With such positive energy flowing after that concert, I was sure things would be good, and I hoped Amelia would feel the same.

217

I looked around and couldn't find Amelia. I stood up on my toes to see if I could find her, but then I heard it. Monica's voice. Monica was standing next to Amelia. Amelia threw her hands up to her head. *Was she crying? Was she upset?* And how had Monica gotten to her before I had? This woman had some serious nerve. She better not have said anything about the sneeze. I walked toward them, clutching the roses so hard I could feel the thorns biting into my fingers.

"And he said he can see me next week?" Amelia asked, her face lit up with hope.

Monica put one manicured hand on Amelia's shoulder possessively. "He can't wait. He's very excited to meet you."

"What's going on?" I asked, pushing in between them. They both turned to stare, and Amelia's face paled.

"Nothing bad, Mom. Monica was telling me—"

"Don't 'nothing Mom' me. I've had enough of this. Monica, where do you get off?"

"Excuse me? Kells, wait a second." Monica took a step back. Conversations among other parents in the lobby died. I could feel their judgmental stares, but I didn't care. Everything was coming to the surface, and there was nothing I could do to stop the words spilling from my lips. This needed to end, *now*.

"First you take Jake's side after I get pregnant, after I told you I considered you my *sister*. My sister. Don't think I haven't seen you on double dates with him and some floozy."

"I didn't—" Monica began, but I cut her off.

"Honestly, I don't care anymore about you being friends with Jake. You can be mean to me, but I won't stand by and watch you mess up my daughter's life."

"Mom. She's not messing up my life," Amelia broke in, tears swelling in her eyes.

"First you convince her to give up on her education. And yes, I came around when it came to the gap year," I went on, ignoring Amelia's interjection.

"I didn't tell her to give up—" Monica began, but I was on a roll. Once this Southern lady got going, there was no stopping her. We've got two sayings in my family: the bigger the hair, the closer to God. The other one? Hell hath no fury like a Raymond woman scorned.

"I don't want to hear any more excuses. What are you doing setting my daughter up on some date with an older man? Trying to distract her from gap year program applications? You've done enough, Monica. The jig is up." I shoved the bouquet into Amelia's hands and pulled her next to me. "Amelia won't be going on any blind dates, and she's going to go to college like we planned. And you can stay out of it, you—you—you sly plotting Grinch."

Monica's jaw dropped. Not a creature was stirring—not a parent, child, or even a mouse in the entire auditorium.

Monica shook her head. "I'm sorry you feel this way, Kells. Believe me, I never wanted to cause you any pain. I guess it's good to know exactly how you feel about me." Tears built in her steel-blue eyes, and she turned on her fancy designer heels and rushed away.

Amelia glared at me. "How could you, Mom?" She threw the bouquet at my Fit and walked away, leaving me stooping to pick up the tangled bundle of flowers with everyone silently watching.

My phone buzzed in my purse. I pulled it out and rushed away from the gawking remnant.

"Georgia," I whispered, cheeks burning and heart thumping. "Just a second." I noticed the art room door was slightly ajar. I slipped in and gently pushed the door shut.

"Please tell me some good news," I said through gritted teeth, trying to swallow the rapidly growing lump in my throat.

"I'm sorry, Kelly Jo—I know this is super late, but I had to tell you. I can't run on Saturday. I found out today at the doctor's office that Gracie has the *chicken pox*, of all things. And she had the vaccination. It's not a bad case, but I guess sometimes kids can still get them, even after the shot. I'm so sorry, Kells."

"Oh, poor sweet Gracie. No worries, Georgia, it's fine," I said.

"But now you don't have three to run. Can you still do it? I know this is horrible timing, but I can't leave Gracie," Georgia said, sounding miserable.

"I understand." I tried to sound soothing, but my voice still shook from the altercation with Monica. "Please tell that little sweet girl of yours I hope she feels better soon." I hung up before my voice could break. I dumped the roses in the trashcan, walked out of the room, and out the back door.

It was bitterly cold in the empty, dark parking lot, and there were none of the sweet, light snowflakes like the ones that had fallen onto the stage. Instead, it looked like it might rain. Cold, icy rain.

I slowly walked back to my truck, the wind making my whole body feel numb. I left my coat unzipped. I deserved to feel the chill.

I climbed into the driver's seat and stared at my phone. Erik would probably never text me again. It was pointless to even check my phone.

I would have chucked it out the window, but I needed to call the radio station and let them know they needed to give our tickets to someone else—a person more deserving. Maybe they would let Fiona run with some other ladies, so then I wouldn't let her down too.

I glanced at my clock on the dashboard. I would have to call them tomorrow. It was already too late tonight. The clock had already struck midnight. Well, nine. This Cinderella had run out of magic before even making it all the way to midnight.

~ Thirty-Two ~

"When I first started running and walking, I would see women wearing spandex pants, and I thought they were crazy. Later, I thought, who cares—wear whatever you want. Be comfortable, and don't worry about it!"
-Beth, runner for three years

I woke up early Friday morning and immediately put on my running clothes. It was a normal thing to do now, practically a habit.

Usually, after such a horrible night, I would eat all my feelings in cookies, ice cream with chocolate syrup, or potato chips. That all sounded amazing, but for some reason, I knew they wouldn't make me feel better this time. The only thing I wanted to do was go for a run.

I laced up my sneakers, adrenaline already at full speed, but paused when I heard a noise from Amelia's room. Weird. She wasn't usually up this early. I tiptoed down the hall, my heart pounding.

"My name is Amelia Raymond, and I'm auditioning for singing talent representation," Amelia said, her voice slightly muffled.

I pushed her door open a crack and peeked in. She stood in front of her mirror and held a hairbrush, her posture pin straight. She opened her mouth and began to sing.

It was a song I hadn't heard before, but it immediately took my breath away. I'd heard Amelia sing pop solos in her a cappella group before, and the one line of "O Holy Night," during dress rehearsal, but when I heard her sing this time all by herself, it was incredible. She had such control over her voice, and a deep, rich tone that reminded me of Adele. I had always been proud of my daughter, I knew she had an amazing voice, but something about hearing her all alone with the perfect choice of song made something click in my mind.

I wasn't proud of her because she was my daughter, and I didn't think she had a great voice because of a mom bias. She was *good*. No, she wasn't just good—she was great and confident.

The minute she finished the song, I pushed the door open. Amelia jumped.

"Mom. I didn't know you were awake."

"Me? What about you?"

She stared at me like she was waiting for a reprimand, but instead I threw my arms around her.

"That was amazing."

"Thank you," she said tentatively, her arms stiff by her side, clearly still worried I would start yelling again. But I was done with all that. I drew back.

"What did you mean when you said you were auditioning for talent representation?"

Amelia frowned. "Mom, you were spying on me?"

"Amelia, I got up and heard something from your room. I was hardly *spying*," I said defensively. I could speak confidently to the fact that I wasn't spying, because I knew exactly what that looked like. Me, crouched in the bushes, eavesdropping on Monica's conversation. My cheeks burned at the memory, and I said quickly, "so, what were you doing?"

"I was practicing. I have an audition," she said slowly. "Monica helped me book it. I tried to tell you last night—she knows this agent, William Putney, and he agreed to let me audition for representation."

I slapped my forehead. "Are you serious? That's the older man?"

"Yeah. Monica called him."

"Monica did that for you?"

"Yeah. He works with a lot of recording studios, and if I do well in the audition, I could have a shot at recording an album with this team that sings and travels for an entire year. Monica thinks I'm a shoe-in."

"So, there's no set up with an older man?" I felt like an idiot. How could I have gotten it all so wrong?

"Moomma," Amelia said, exasperated, "I'm not trying to *date* an older man—I'm trying to get one to *represent* me."

I threw my hand over my mouth and muffled a groan. "Oh, sweetie. I'm so sorry. I'm sorry about everything." Everything was finally making sense. I felt terribly guilty for jumping to such crazy conclusions. My apology tumbled out. "I was so pushy about you going to college that I never stopped to think if it was truly the right thing for you. I know we talked, but after hearing you sing just now, I feel like I finally woke up and saw what was really going on. You're so talented. You have a real shot at this, don't you?"

"I think I do," Amelia said, smiling up at me. "And I know you want the best for me, Momma." She reached up and grabbed my hand.

"I can't believe Monica helped you with the gap year, and now with this. She was more supportive than I've been." I squeezed her hand. "I haven't helped you at all. I'm so sorry that I didn't believe in you like I should've. And I was horrible to Monica. I thought she was the wicked witch, but it turns out, it was me all along. I'm the unreliable character."

Amelia squeezed my hand back and said softly, "Maybe Monica arranged the actual auditions, but you're the one who inspired me to actually pursue all of this, Momma."

"I've only held you back," I insisted, but Amelia shook her head.

"With all this stuff you've been doing with running, Momma, you're fearless. Seeing you train for this 5K inspired me to book these auditions," she continued. "I booked them even though I wasn't sure I could go. Just like you, Momma. You aren't sure if you can finish the 5K or not, but you just went for it. Monica sorted out the details, but *you're* the reason I had the guts to do it in the first place."

I pulled her into a bear hug. "Amelia, I'm so proud of you. Do you know that?" She reached around and wrapped her arms around me, too.

Amelia may have said that I inspired her, but in that moment, she *inspired me*. And I knew exactly what to do. I was tired of being a horrible person.

"Keep practicing, Amelia. I've got something to do that is long overdue." I leaned down, tied my sneakers in double knots, and raced out the door.

~ * ~

Monica's house was perfect, just like I remembered, as I ran up to it, slightly sweaty despite the freezing cold. Maybe I should have driven, but I had so much energy after my heart-to-heart with Amelia that I wanted to run it out.

When I reached the front steps, I halted. What if Monica slammed the door in my face? *I* would do that if I were her, after everything I said to her last night.

Before I could talk myself out of it, and imagine

225

any horrible scenarios, I knocked on her door. After a moment, she opened it cautiously. She wore a pristine white blouse with a little snowflake brooch, put together as always, but she seemed slightly wilted.

"Kelly Jo? What are you doing here?"

I stepped inside the door before she could shut it on me, and I hugged her. She was going to have to deal with all the sweat on her perfect outfit.

"Monica, you're an angel."

"This is—unexpected," she said, confused.

I broke away, almost laughing at her befuddled expression. I pulled off my knitted hat and twisted it in my hands. "I'm so sorry for everything I said to you. I'm sorry I called you a sly plotting Grinch. I'm sorry for everything. Amelia told me about the audition you helped book for her. I was so mean to you, but all along you've done nothing but look out for my daughter. How can I ever make it up to you?"

Monica's face relaxed when she realized I wasn't there to yell at her. She closed the door behind me. "Why don't you come inside for a cup of coffee?"

I followed her in and sat down at her kitchen table. She placed a mug covered with little angels holding Christmas stars in front of me, which seemed very apropos, and poured me a steaming mug of coffee.

"Kelly, I'm really sorry," she said, pouring herself a cup and then sitting right next to me. "I have wanted so badly to talk to you. I think what started all of this was that it looked like I basically took Jake's side when he left you—you know, back in college?"

I took a sip of the coffee. That was certainly true.

"I was a hot mess, Kelly Jo," she said, clutching her mug. "I really didn't want to go on double dates with Jake and forget you, but my husband worked with him. Michael said he needed Jake by his side to work his way up the corporate ladder. I hated it, but I was newly married, and young and stupid. I truly hated it, Kells. I never should have listened to him. I've missed you so much. I wanted to reach out to you, but I just didn't know how, so I reached out to Amelia instead." She stared into her coffee and drew in a breath. "Besides, you have such amazing friends now. You totally upgraded, and I knew you couldn't stand me anymore, but I wanted to at least try to help Amelia, to make up for what I've done to you. And Kelly Jo, she really *is* talented."

"Upgraded? Monica, you're hardly an outdated model," I said quickly. I never knew that a woman so put together like Monica could still feel self-conscious, but when I watched her squirm in front of me, I realized that she was just as insecure as I was sometimes.

"That's how I felt," she said finally. "I guess I thought that if I helped your daughter, maybe you might forgive me. Besides, Amelia's so talented, I was happy to do what I could to help her career. But everything I do keeps getting twisted."

"Monica, I'm sorry for everything. Do you think you can forgive me?" I looked over into her eyes and grabbed tightly to the lil' mug with both hands.

Monica broke into a smile. "Me forgive you? I want you to forgive me. You don't know how much I've missed you, Kells."

I set aside my mug and drew her into a hug once more, and this time, she squeezed me just as tightly.

227

~ Thirty-Three ~

"If this is your first race, do the best you can and just finish. Run at your own pace, and don't compare yourself to others. Find someone else to run with. It makes running so much better."
—Tanya, runner for twenty-two years

The stage director had a breakdown about the a cappella performance and persuaded Monica to hold a second dress rehearsal that Wednesday night. Apparently, the snowflakes weren't "just right," and he was concerned about coordinating some last-minute song changes with the prop and curtain stage managers.

"I'm not going to complain," I told Amelia while I drove over to the auditorium. We could've used some of that fake snow outside to create a better ambiance. The sky was dark, and it was freezing, but there were no pretty flakes to be seen. "I'm excited I get to hear you sing *O Holy Night* again. Besides, I think we all need second chances."

"If I sneeze again, I'm going to be humiliated. So, I guess extra practice is good. But maybe this time, don't yell at Monica in front of all the parents?" She raised her brow, and I cringed.

"I'm so sorry. I probably have quite a reputation now."

Monica might be okay with me, but parents probably still had crazy opinions about me after my scene the other night. I didn't even want to think about what kind of rumors they had started. *That* was gossip best unimagined.

"They already thought you were a sassy Southerner with an attitude," Amelia said, and I patted my hair.

"I am a Southern woman. I raise h-e-double hockey sticks if need be."

"Momma, seriously? Are you sure you can contain yourself?" Amelia laughed, nudging my shoulder.

"I'll do my best," I said, pulling into the parking lot. I shivered, already feeling the chill seeping through the windows once the heat cut off. "By the way, since I never got to give you your flowers the other night, I have something for you."

"What is it?" she asked, looking around the backseat for another bouquet. I pulled an envelope out of my purse.

She tore it open and examined the contents. "Plane tickets?"

"Since you're probably going to be traveling around the world touring with some amazing gap year tour group, I thought we'd take a trip of our own first...to Hawaii," I said, beaming. "A week of reading on the beach, riding bikes, and drinking cold iced tea by the ocean—and maybe one or two delicious drinks in those coconut shells with the little umbrellas—for *me* of course. What do you think? After all, I want to spend time with you before you become a star and get too busy."

Amelia stared at me, speechless. I bit my lip.

"You don't want to go? Amelia, I can return them if you don't."

She suddenly shrieked in excitement. "I'm going to Hawaii! Mele Kalikimaka is the thing to say on a bright Hawaiian Christmas day..." she began to sing.

229

She pulled me into a hug. "Momma, thank you so much. And I promise I'll always have time for you, even when I'm a star. You have to come to the Grammys with me, we can get amazing dresses and a limo."

We walked arm and arm up to the front of the school. I was so warm inside I hardly noticed the chill.

When we got into the building, all the members of the a cappella group were gathered in front of the auditorium. They talked to a tall, chiseled man.

My heart suddenly raced as if I were running up the steepest hill in all of Kentucky. "Erik?"

"What's he doing here?" Amelia whispered.

"Kelly Jo Raymond," he said, his face turning pale when he spotted me. "What are you doing here?"

"I was going to ask you the same question," I said, confused. Why on earth was *he* turning pale? Was there already another woman, and he didn't know how to break it to me? I *knew* I screwed up that date. It wasn't my crazy imagination. It was a good thing Amelia and I were arm in arm, because she was practically holding me up.

"I had to come back from Texas from my business meeting," Erik said. "There was an emergency. My construction team is doing some work next door. I was talking to the group earlier. I'm so sorry, but unfortunately we're going to have to evacuate this area for a week." He ran a hand through his hair nervously.

"Tomorrow's show is postponed," one of the parents said, clearly annoyed. "Of all things, leave it to this town."

"You mean the kids can't perform *tomorrow*

230

night?" I asked, my heartbeat quickening. "There's no holiday concert tomorrow night? Not at all?"

"No, it's not safe," Erik said. "There's a gas leak next door, and they're worried about the kids here. I already spoke to the superintendent of schools. We must shut down this area for at least a couple of days, which means the performance can only take place once the area is clear. Your daughter is in the group, right? I'm so sorry." He looked miserable, but I threw my arms around him and kissed him right on the lips before he could finish.

When I pulled away, he looked confused. My cheeks burned. Why had I done that? The man wasn't interested anymore, hadn't texted me in forever, so I needed to just take a hint. Sure, he hadn't pushed me away during the kiss, but he hadn't reciprocated, which could only mean that he didn't like me the way I liked him.

Amelia stared at us, shocked.

"Um, that was just my way of saying thanks," I said, then pulled Amelia away before Erik could respond. I had suddenly regained control of my legs, and I needed to get out of there immediately.

"At least you didn't yell at anyone this time," Amelia whispered to me, amused. "I didn't think to add 'don't randomly make out with someone' on the list of things to avoid."

"Very funny," I said, dying of embarrassment.

I may have messed that up, I thought, *but I have bigger fish to fry—namely, a race with a certain country star.*

As I walked outside, arm in arm with my warrior princess daughter, I pulled out my phone and shot off a text to Monica:

> *Call me tonight.*
> *I have a crazy idea.*

~ Thirty-Four ~

"One of my best memories at a race is of my husband and my kids. Just after the start of the race, coming around a corner, I saw my husband jumping as high as he could, throwing both arms into the air and screaming my name, 'Debbie. Go Debbie! Go!' He was completely abandoned to encouragement."
-Debbie, runner for fifteen years.

There were huge groups of people gathered around in red and green tutus, Santa and elf outfits, and even a full nativity scene with running shoes. And everyone, as per the race suggestions, wore jingle bells on their race bibs. The crowd sounded like a thousand little Santa sleighs.

A woman with a jingle bell tag around her neck that said "Kim" motioned for Fiona, Amelia, Shruti, and me to follow her. "Ladies, please follow me to the front of the line."

She smiled and continued. "Shruti, you can stand over there, and Fiona and Kelly Jo, we need to line up now. It's about time for Drake to—" she broke off, lost in her own flurry of preparation. She was a woman of order, I could tell, and I liked her immediately.

Shruti scooted over to the side with her crutches. She was fast. She easily wove her way through the crowd to move to the front.

"Can we wait a few more minutes?" I inter-rupted. "We're waiting on just one more person." I

232

shuffled around trying to see through all the people.

I spotted her in the distance. "Monica. Monica, we're over here." I waved like a giant windmill trying to catch her attention through the crowd.

Monica joined the group, looking out-of-place for once. She wore a simple red running shirt and black pants. I pulled her into our clique and handed her a red and green tutu. I had made them the night before, with Amelia's help. She was on the sidelines, wearing a matching one to cheer us on.

"This is Kim, our handler," I told Monica. "She's in charge of introducing us to Drake. And this is Fiona. Oh, and Shruti, too—she's over there watching from the sidelines." I looked at everyone, tears welling up in my eyes. "Y'all, I'm so glad everyone is here with me. Even though I've been so horrible lately." I looked up to heaven and shot up a quick prayer for forgiveness—and thankfulness. My heart was full.

"Kelly Jo, what in the world? This is amazing," Fiona said. I had never seen her so excited.

"Yes," Monica said, laughing at Fiona's exuberance. "It is amazing. Thank you, Kells."

"Thank *you*." I beamed at Monica. It was just like old times. "Look at everyone looking at us," I said, nodding at the crowd.

"This is better than anything I could imagine," someone whispered when they passed us.

"Those are the contest winners," another runner said. "They get to meet Drake. I'm so jealous."

"This is crazy." I said breathlessly. "I can't believe that we, that you, that I..."

"It's really happening," Monica said, looping her arm through mine. "And everyone watching is probably dying of jealousy. 'Look at that sexy woman who's about to meet Drake Douglas.'" She winked.

"The woman with the sexy legs," Fiona said.

"Sexy legs that are freezing cold." I laughed, jumping up and down a bit. It was so cold that I could see my breath come out in icy puffs, even though I was bundled up in a base layer, the tutu, and a red sequin-covered Santa hat. I looked around at my friends. They were dressed in similarly hilarious but festive outfits. I sent up another quick prayer. *Thank you, God. I am truly blessed.*

Just then, a huge black limo pulled over and Drake Douglas stepped out. He was tall, dark, and yes, he was *oh so easy* on the eyes. He wore an all-black, expensive-looking running outfit, topped off with a red and green cowboy hat. I lost my breath for a second, and we hadn't even started running yet.

Everyone in the crowd started screaming.

"Ladies and gentlemen, Drake Douglas has arrived," the emcee called over a microphone. "The race will begin in three minutes."

I glanced around the crowd and saw Shruti standing with Amelia. Shruti raised her crutch and waved it in the air. I waved and blew them both kisses. I felt like a movie star.

Drake Douglas sauntered slowly to the front of the line, shaking hands and thanking people for coming out for the fundraiser. He walked right to us. I was fixated on his eyes. He had clear, beautiful, sunny-sky-day-blue-eyes.

"And who, may I ask, is Kelly Jo Raymond?" he said in his deep drawl, and my heart beat wildly.

"That's me," I said, raising my hand straight up in the air.

"It's so good to meet you, Miss Kelly Jo."

He reached up, gently took my hand and then he gallantly pressed his lips to the back of my glove. I nearly melted.

He looked over toward Monica and Fiona. "And these women are...?"

"These are my dear friends, Monica and Fiona," I said, and they each gave a little wave, totally star struck and totally unable to hide it.

"Ladies, I'm so thankful you're here today to run with me. I'm a bit out of shape. I hope I can keep up." He winked at me.

"That's a relief, because this is the first 5K I have ever run in my life."

"Same." He laughed. He shot a second look at Fiona, holding her gaze. "What about you? This isn't your first rodeo, is it?"

She stared at him, and then seemed to process his words. "I've never been in a rodeo," she said, dazed.

He grinned. "What about a 5k?"

"I've done that," she said, eyes widening, "but I can't remember when. For some reason I suddenly can't remember a thing," Fiona said.

I threw my hand over my mouth to stop myself from laughing right out loud. I had never seen Fiona flustered before, and right now, talking to Drake Douglas, she was most *definitely* flustered. Her cheeks were bright red, and not just from the cold.

"Ladies and gentlemen take your places at the start," the emcee called. "The Jingle Bell Run begins in ten, nine..."

Everyone around us joined in with the count.

"Let's do this run," Drake said. He bent slightly and leaned forward.

"...Two, one, GO!" the emcee yelled.

We were off. My heart raced, and my legs took off running faster than I usually started any run, but hallelujah, I didn't pull a Laura Beth and break limbs at the start line.

Several people wove in and around us. A woman with a jogging stroller sped right by. A guy in a furry polar bear costume passed us.

Drake and Fiona naturally fell into a great pace together, and Monica and I followed close behind. Along the way, we heard jingle bells ringing, groups of people singing Drake's song, and even saw people holding up signs of encouragement along the way with phrases like "You can do it" and "Jingle all the way to the finish line." Some held cups of steaming hot chocolate, but for once, I didn't wish I was on the sidelines downing a sweet drink. I was right where I belonged.

I couldn't believe it when we reached the first mile. It seemed like the best mile I had ever run, and I was still feeling great. I was getting into this groove of breathing and running, and it felt amazing.

The race continued like a dream. We all ran in a group, staying close to Drake, with Fiona right at his side.

Mile two felt a bit longer than the first. I caught myself holding my breath a few times, and I had to remind myself to *just breathe.*

We turned around a corner in the street, which meant that we were already halfway done and on our way back. It felt much faster than our training 5K, and I closed my eyes for a moment, memorizing everything.

We raced up a long slow hill. When we reached the top, I could see the finish line banner at the bottom of the hill, covered in twinkling Christmas lights. The crowds cheered, and I was shocked to find I had more energy than I had ever felt by the end of any workout.

"Let's show them what we've got on this last stretch, ladies," Drake said, and he picked up the pace.

Racing toward the finish line was more exhilarating than fighting off crowds to get sixty percent off Kate Spade™ purses at the outlets. It was even more exciting than Black Friday, Hunter Boots™, or anything chocolate. I could hardly breathe, and my chest was heaving, but I was almost done. I could push through. I just knew it.

The. Finish. Line. Was. In. Sight.

When we approached the finish line, I grabbed Monica's hand on one side and Fiona's hand on the other. Fiona reached over and grabbed Drake's hand. We threw up our arms in the air and all crossed the finish line together, as if we were a team of actors and we had practiced our final curtain call for weeks.

But it was better than being onstage with my hair teased to high heaven, wearing sequins. And after all, it was real, and it was perfect.

"This is the dreamiest 5K ever," I said.

I looked around the crowd of people on the sidelines and sure enough, Shruti was there, waving her crutch in the air. And Amelia was jumping up and down waving at us all. Monica's daughter Lindsay was there now, too. They all wore our signature red and green tutus and were screaming, cheering, waving and running toward us. At Drake. At *me*.

"You did it, Mom. You're amazing."

She handed me a plastic cup of water. "Is Erik here, too?"

I felt a tiny pang of sadness.

"I don't think that's happening anymore, sweetie," I said, downing my water and wiping sweat off my brow. "Things have been awkward between us. I don't think he likes me anymore—I screwed up."

"Oh, okay," Amelia said, looking crestfallen.

"What is it, hon?" I turned and tossed my empty water cup in the recycling bin.

"What happened to Raymond women knowing what they want and going for it?" Amelia asked, a familiar spark in her eye. I realized where I had seen it before. I had that same spark now.

"Why Amelia Sue Raymond, what are you suggestin'? Are you suggestin' I go find this cowboy of mine and lasso him in here and now in front of God and everyone?"

Monica walked up behind me. "Why not, Kells? He lives in Lexington, right?"

I glanced around at the buildings all around us. "Actually...I don't think he lives very far from here."

"Well," Amelia said, "are you up for a little victory lap?"

I felt a rush of panic and excitement rise in my stomach. It was a crazy idea. I couldn't run to Erik's place after completing a 5K.

The normal thing to do would be to wait until he responded. That's what the old Kelly Jo would do. But the new Kelly Jo wore broken-in running shoes, a sequin hat and jingle bells, and she had just enough determination left to accomplish the task.

I glanced up at Amelia and Monica, took in a deep breath, and grinned.

"Be right back."

I jogged off, and heard Fiona yell after me,

"Drake says he has an extra concert ticket..."

~ * ~

There was a stitch in my side and my legs were exhausted, but I felt a new surge of adrenaline while I soared through my victory mile. The tinkling sound of the jingle bells kept me going, a little rhythm like a Christmasy heartbeat. By the time I arrived at Erik's house, I was exhausted.

I went all the way to his front door then paused to catch my breath. For a moment I just stared at the Christmas wreath hanging there. It was a cluster of pinecones, and I leaned forward and smelled the musky scent. It reminded me of him, and my knees wobbled.

"You can do this," I whispered, then raised my hand and knocked. I was so nervous I couldn't stand still, even though I was completely exhausted. No answer. I knocked again.

Just my luck. He wasn't home.

I looked up to heaven, raised my hands, and shrugged my shoulders. *I tried.*

Suddenly I heard music in the background. It was Drake's song, *"Running to your Dreams."* It came from Erik's back porch.

I jogged around the house and found Erik sitting on his porch swing, bundled up in a thick flannel coat and holding a mug of mulled cider.

"Hey," I said quietly.

"Kelly Jo," he said, standing in surprise. "Aren't you running your race?"

"Just ran it," I said, and I struck a pose in my sweat-covered running outfit, and my bells jingled. "And then, I thought I'd run a little extra."

"I'm confused." He shifted his weight from one foot to another. "Why are you here?"

"I really like you," I said, my heart beating faster, even though I stood still. "I thought things were going well, but then you stopped talking to me. Are you not interested? I guess I'd just rather know. But I also wanted to be up front with you and tell you that I *am* interested. I'm *very* interested in—" I gestured to his whole body. He had a stupefied expression. "—in all of this."

"I'm interested in all of this," he said and gestured at all of me, in my sweaty workout gear, wilted tutu, and the Santa hat that kept flopping into my eyes. "And everything inside that lovely mind of yours, too. I think you're amazing. I always have."

"Really?" I said softly, unable to think of a better response. I held myself back from making finger guns and saying *then let's get out of this town, together, cowboy.* Instead I blurted, "So, why the cold shoulder? You know, in the truck? And why haven't you been texting me?"

"At the restaurant I saw you taking photos of your ex," he said, looking sheepish. "It just got in my head. I made up this whole story where I thought you were still in love with him, and that was all I could think about."

"In love with my ex? Oh, my heavens, no. I was taking pictures because he was with my former friend, Monica, who's now my friend again. It's kind of a lot to explain. But trust me, I only have eyes for you." I swatted him on the arm. "Sounds like you have an overactive imagination."

"Maybe we have that in common."

"Are you busy tonight?" I whispered. "I happen to have an extra ticket to a pretty awesome concert."

Erik didn't wait for me to finish. He caught my hand and pulled me into a soft embrace, bent down, and kissed my lips.

"So, should I put you down for a 'maybe' to go to the concert?"

"Put me down as a definite yes," he whispered.

And somehow, at that moment, it began to snow.

~ Thirty-Five ~

"Just minutes after I cross a finish line, I'm thinking about the next race, and what I'll do differently or the same—even if during the last mile of the race I said to myself, 'What was I thinking—I'm dying here!' Those strong feelings just disappear. I can't explain it."
-Cheryl, runner for twenty-six years

I opened the door to Main and Maple and rushed inside. My new sneakers squeaked when I slipped on coffee drips on the floor, but this time I didn't fall. I didn't hit anyone, and I didn't spill anything on anyone.

I waved at Shruti, Fiona, Georgia, and Monica sitting in our chairs at the back of the coffee shop. They waved back.

"So glad you're here, Kells," Shruti said. Her leg was stretched straight out, crutches placed neatly on the floor beside her. "Your text said you have big news made. I'm curious."

"How do your legs feel, Kells?" Fiona cut in. "I can't believe I wasn't sore."

"I was," I said, and everyone chuckled. I pulled out my chair, sat down, and crossed my legs. I couldn't stop bouncing my leg.

"You're so cheery," Shruti observed. "Did you already have a few cups of coffee?"

"Nope," I said placing both legs on the floor and leaning back in my chair. "I still have leftover adrenaline from the race."

"From a week ago?" Shruti asked tilting her head.

"Yes. I could get used to this. I feel more pumped up than when I'm shopping."

"Running together has been so much fun this fall," Fiona said. "I'm so glad you talked us into it."

"So am I, even if that little dog put a damper on things," Shruti said, and pointed at her leg.

"And a crazy case of chicken pox."

"And a few misunderstandings." I glanced at Monica.

"Thank you again for letting me run with you," Monica said, smiling warmly at me. "I haven't had that much fun in about eighteen years."

"I never knew I loved country music so much," Fiona said, sipping her coffee primly.

I laughed. I knew it wasn't really the music Fiona was enamored with, but the musician. It was Drake Douglas, with his sweet disposition and dreamy eyes.

"I can't believe we got to spend so much time with Drake. He really is an incredible musician," Monica said, reading my mind. "Oh, and Kells, this came in the mail at school today." Monica handed me a huge envelope with Amelia's name written on the front.

The sender was the gap year choir program, the program Amelia had auditioned for.

"What do you think it means?" I asked.

"I've never known a thick envelope like this to mean a no," Monica said with a smile. "Looks like Amelia will be heading to Europe for a year of singing."

I couldn't breathe. The news stopped my heart. She did it. My girl—my *young lady*—had done it. Her dreams were coming true. *Thank you, Lord.*

"Hooray for Amelia," Fiona cheered.

We held up our coffee mugs, clunked them together, and cheered for Amelia. I settled back in the seat and took a sip of my skinny peppermint latte.

Georgia leaned in. "So, Kelly Jo, what was the news you were so excited about?"

"I almost forgot." I said, licking whipped cream off my lips. "If we can accomplish so much by training for a 5K, imagine what else we can do. I'm going back to get my degree. And I finished the race, even though I never thought I could. And now that Amelia will be gone shortly, I'll have even *more* time for all these goals—"

"Kells, where in the world are you going with this? Spit it out, girlfriend," Georgia said sternly.

"Let's go for the next big dream." I paused for a bit of dramatic effect and took a deep breath. "A 10K, ladies. A 10K."

Monica was the first to raise her coffee mug. "I'm in."

Fiona, Shruti, and Georgia raised their mugs.

I raised mine and clinked it with theirs. "Here's to amazing friends, a new year, and a new dream."

~ END ~

Jingle Bell Run   Pamela Seales